# THE STORIES OF OUR LIVES

### A Short Story Collection

## BRANDY ISADORA

Published by Brandimar

Library of Congress Control Number: 2021903768

ISBN 978-1-7335820-2-5

*In memory of Dorien Ross*

# CONTENTS

| | |
|---|---|
| Bundle & Save | 1 |
| The Weight of Sound | 10 |
| Rumors and Secrets | 16 |
| Cloudburst | 20 |
| Human Cannonball | 40 |
| Extras | 49 |
| The Three Phillies | 58 |
| Holy Water | 73 |
| Around the Fur | 82 |
| Fifty-Five & Older | 87 |
| The Lovetts | 117 |
| Gunsmoke | 123 |
| Where the Animals Roam | 133 |
| Ava | 152 |
| The Preacher | 163 |
| A Place of Their Own | 175 |
| Wanderlust | 184 |
| Real Man | 202 |
| A Note from the author | 211 |
| About the Author | 213 |

# BUNDLE & SAVE

Inside Lucky's Pub, Mitch McKinley's gaze switched between his cold glass of beer sweating droplets and the laundromat directly across the street. Tonight, he felt no interest in the basketball game playing on the television at the bar.

Since his retirement two years ago as a high school chemistry teacher, Mitch's life had been pared down to restoring his three-bedroom home in the Garfield Historic District and hanging out at Lucky's Pub, consuming two pints of beer and watching whatever sports event was playing on the television that night. Since his wife's passing five years before, Mitch had a hard time sleeping, so he would walk the fourteen blocks from his home to the bar to take his mind off of life, and then he would walk back home again.

If anyone had asked him, he would say he felt content with his life. He got used to having more free time and spending time alone, which is why he appreciated this particular pub. The place was never crowded, though it had its handful of regular patrons. After spending thirty-plus years handling teenagers who preferred to do anything else but chemistry

1

homework, Mitch preferred his solitude. He didn't hate people, but he now kept his distance from most of them. His wife, Susan, had been the social one. The only company he kept these days was Lucy, a German Shepherd named after his favorite actress, Lucille Ball. His wife would have appreciated that.

Mitch's eyes narrowed, even though he could easily read the neon blue and purple letters from across the street that read "Bundle & Save." Their parking lot was starting to fill up with cars. A man and a woman, who got out of separate cars, embraced each other and appeared to exchange a few words before walking into the laundromat. The man looked to be in his late fifties, while the woman seemed at least a couple decades younger.

Mitch glanced at his watch. It was 9:30 p.m. on a Friday night.

"How long has that place been open?" Mitch asked the bartender, tilting his head toward the window.

"The laundromat?" The bartender set down the pitcher he was washing and leaned over the bar to look out the window. "Maybe a month now."

"It seems weird that so many people would be going to a laundromat on a Friday night. Have you ever been there?"

"Nope. I've got a unit in my apartment. That's always been a deal breaker for me. I gotta have my own washer and dryer." The bartender immediately went back to cleaning the plastic beer pitchers.

Mitch continued watching the activity at the laundromat as he finished his glass. More cars showed up and before long, there were no parking spots left. Mitch sat at the bar, dividing his attention between the television, his beer, and the laundromat. Not everyone displayed affection for each other, but their facial expressions suggested that they were familiar with each other.

There's something strange going on with that place, Mitch thought. He finally got tired of sitting and paid his tab and left the bar.

For the next week, Mitch went to the bar every night to watch the comings and goings at the laundromat. Every night more and more cars started filling up the parking lot and then the side residential roads. People started showing up around 9:00 p.m. and many stayed past the time Mitch left the bar. Some of the people carried large laundry bags, while others only used small grocery bags. A few didn't even carry any laundry. Now, that seemed unusual for a laundromat, Mitch thought to himself. Maybe Bundle & Save was a front for a far more sinister operation.

Mitch had never seen a laundromat that was so consistently full every night. He wasn't exactly sure why he was so interested in the silly place. It was none of his business, but that didn't stop him from obsessing about the laundromat. Every night he sat in the same seat at the end of the bar, which gave him a perfect view of the building. He was too far away to see things perfectly, but it was enough to nag at him.

"How come you're not out with your wife on Valentine's Day?" The bartender asked Mitch in a tone that was more facetious than serious.

"My wife passed away five years ago," Mitch said softly, glancing down at his wedding band. He hadn't felt ready to take off his ring. The thin, beveled gold band felt like a part of his body.

"I'm sorry, sir. I was out of line." The bartender offered one on the house.

"Don't worry about it," Mitch replied, but he accepted the offer.

"What was her name?"

"Susan. You know, if she were still alive, she'd probably be happy that I spent a little time here. I wasn't the easiest man to live with, and she was quite content having her own space." Mitch smiled thinking of his wife occasionally persuading him to take a fishing trip with a friend so she could have the weekend to herself.

"That laundromat has been doing quite a business since they opened," the bartender said as he mixed a White Russian for another patron at the bar.

"Some of them don't even have anything on them to wash. Something suspicious is going on in that place," Mitch retorted. He paid his tab and went home, feeling an inexplicable irritation toward Bundle & Save.

For two days Mitch stayed at home, working on retiling the guest bathroom. By the third day, he felt like he would lose his mind. As he was cleaning up for the day, his doorbell rang. His twenty-eight-year-old daughter, Chelsea, stood at the front door. Her naturally blond hair was dyed a deep shade of violet. Chelsea worked as a makeup artist, and she frequently experimented with different hair colors. By now Mitch was used to seeing his daughter sporting vibrant colored hair. In fact, if she did show up in her natural hair color, he would think that something was wrong.

"Dad, do you still have that box of mine from the old house? I think it says 'Chelsea's Notebooks.'"

"I'm sure it's here. I put your boxes in the spare bedroom." Mitch led the way to the back bedroom. "I just finished my work for the day. Would you like to go out to dinner tonight?"

"Sorry, Dad. I can't. I'm having a girls' night with Tonya and Kelly. We're checking out a new sushi restaurant."

"Oh. That's nice, sweetheart." Mitch tried to hide his disappointment. Even though Chelsea only lived twenty minutes away, they rarely spent much time together. He didn't fault her for not having the time to see him, but he felt sad they were not as close as they once were.

Sure enough the box was in the spare bedroom, beneath several unpacked boxes of miscellaneous stuff Mitch still had to sort through. Chelsea left as soon as she confirmed she had the right box. She even kissed him on the cheek. That helped.

He took a shower and changed into clean clothes. He grabbed a beer from the fridge and tried to relax watching television. He flipped through the channels indifferently. At one point, Lucy demanded his attention, and he took her for a walk to kill more time. When he returned home, it was completely dark outside. As he flipped the lights on in the kitchen, he saw the pile of dirty laundry sitting on top of the kitchen table. He took a deep breath and stood still for a moment, feeling surprised with himself that he felt so drawn to that darn place. Resigned, he grabbed a plastic shopping bag to carry the small pile of clothes.

When he pulled up to Bundle & Save, he started to question his sanity. He had a perfectly functional washer and dryer. There was no need to hang out in a laundromat for a couple of hours on a Thursday night. He pushed the glass door open and then quickly drew his hand back. This is crazy, he thought. He backed away from the door, nearly bulldozing the woman just behind him.

"Excuse me! I'm so sorry," Mitch apologized to a petite woman. He held the door open for her. "I'm really sorry."

"We don't bite," the woman said.

For a moment, Mitch just stood there transfixed. The rows of mint green washing machines and dryers glistened beneath the soft pink lighting. Small, metal square tables sat between the washers and dryers. Most of them were occupied with other patrons. Mitch recovered from his shock and stepped inside. The machines produced a low hum that slightly drowned the house music. He saw the woman he nearly knocked over walk toward another woman with a platinum blond ponytail. The two women hugged, and then the woman with the bouncing ponytail walked through a door that said Employees Only.

Mitch found an available machine toward the back of the room. Even though the machine looked like an older model, the washer looked clean and well maintained. He put some coins in the machine and dropped a detergent tab into the pile of laundry.

Since there was no room at any of the tables, he leaned against the machine and observed the other customers, who appeared to be a motley group of people of different ages. Mitch could never imagine these people gravitating toward each other outside of this building. Then he noticed it.

Every table was occupied and covered with a board game, some crafting project, or a puzzle. At the table closest to him sat three men finishing a game of Monopoly. He couldn't tell if they all knew each other. Two of them looked to be about his daughter's age, while the third seemed about ten years older than the other two guys. One of the young men had the bottom of his head shaved, while the top of his head was covered with chin-length hair dyed a rather noxious shade of lime green. He wore thick, silver gauges in his ears. In comparison, the other two men looked rather ordinary in their dark-colored sweats and uncolored hair.

Leaning against the washing machine with his hands in his pockets, Mitch observed them until one of them noticed him.

"You want to join us? We're thinking about starting a game of Clue." It was the young man with the green hair who spoke.

"No. That's okay. Thanks anyhow," Mitch responded, feeling slightly embarrassed for being caught staring.

Now the other two men were looking at him. The older one started packing up the Monopoly game into the worn box. He held the pewter figurine of the dog between his index finger and thumb.

"When I was a kid, my little sister accidentally swallowed this and we spent the entire night sitting in the ER. She's a sweet person now, but back then she'd try to eat anything that didn't eat her first."

"Is this your first time here?" The guy with the green hair asked Mitch.

"Yeah. Can't say I've ever been to a laundromat quite like this," Mitch answered. "It seems like a popular hangout."

"You know there's another room back there where they play movies the whole night. There's a bunch of chairs and couches." The guy nodded toward a door across the room that separated a row of dryers.

"Maybe I'll check it out," Mitch said.

The three guys went back to playing another board game. Mitch looked around the laundromat. He wasn't used to leaving anything of his unattended, but this time he really didn't feel concerned that anyone would take his belongings. Besides, he only had a couple of navy-blue Hanes T-shirts and two pairs of jeans that were so old and worn that he actually wouldn't have cared if someone took them.

When Mitch entered the darkened room where the television was playing, a few people turned to look at him. He quietly closed the door and stood transfixed as he saw at least a dozen people sitting on chairs and on the floor wrapped in fleece blankets. He felt rather out of place, but he braved his discomfort and found a place to sit next to a woman who was sipping a Big Slurp. She casually smiled when he sat down.

"Alison at the counter has blankets if you want one," the woman said.

"That's okay. I'm not sure how long I'll be staying," Mitch responded stiffly. He wasn't sure anymore what he was doing, and he started to feel like he had entered another world.

He recognized the movie on the screen. They were watching *Back to the Future*. Mitch actually remembered watching that film with his wife when it had originally played in the theaters. Maybe he would be staying longer than he thought.

"Would you like a snickerdoodle?" The woman held up a Tupperware filled with cookies. Even though her face was plain, there was a warmth in her eyes. Her mouth slightly turned upward, which made her seem more approachable to Mitch. "I bake pastries for a pizza shop, so you can trust me that they're really good."

"Um, sure. Thank you." Mitch reluctantly took one of the cookies. He didn't really have much of a sweet tooth, but he didn't want to offend the woman.

Mitch was surprised at how good the cookie tasted. It was the perfect amount of sweetness for him. The combination of the snickerdoodle and movie seemed to put Mitch in a serene state of mind. He allowed himself to enjoy the scene, and he completely forgot about his laundry and his life, which had become more and more empty as he lost the things he loved most in the world.

He suddenly felt a hand lay ever so gently on his back and he jolted from the shock. He looked over his shoulder to see the woman with the ponytail holding a blanket.

"I'm so sorry! I didn't mean to scare you. I just wanted to know if you'd like a blanket," she said.

"Sure," he answered. He wasn't even cold, but there was something appealing to him about having the soft fleece against his skin.

The woman unfolded the blanket and carefully wrapped it

around his shoulders. Without another word, the woman left the room.

The woman sitting next to Mitch leaned toward him. "That's Alison. She's the owner of the laundromat."

"She certainly knows how to run a busy laundromat," he whispered.

"Alison had a son who fought in Iraq. When he got back, he suffered badly from PTSD. He had a hard time sleeping, and one night he took his life. She started this place for people who suffer from insomnia. The nights are the hardest, sometimes."

Mitch nodded, feeling both speechless and stunned. His eyes blurred as a stubborn, watery film covered his eyes. He coughed and quickly brushed his hand over his eyes.

"The nights are the hardest," Mitch whispered. He could feel the woman looking at him before she put her hand on his forearm.

"That's why we're all here. We get it," she said.

Part of him wanted to laugh at himself, even though his eyes were still moist. He had thought the worst of these people at first, and now he realized he felt more connected to these strangers in a way that he had never felt before.

They went back to watching the movie, and for a couple of hours Mitch forgot what it felt like to be alone.

# THE WEIGHT OF SOUND

## Warsaw, Poland

*Greta and Hanna*

I stood outside the small convenience store smoking a cigarette while Hanna grabbed some goodies for the park. When she came out, she held the bag open in front of me so I could stare at the pile of candy bars, chips, and soda. I dipped my hand into the bag and snatched some chocolate. I was starving.

We sat in our usual place at the park, near the thick rows of trees that border the flawless lawn. We just wanted to be left alone to do our own thing, smoke, talk, and devour candy. Hanna took off her bright green faux fur coat and put it on the ground before sitting. She pulled out a soda and powered up her laptop so she could play her music.

"Is something going on here today? Why are people bringing ice chests? It's not a holiday." I started twirling my hair between my fingers, a tendency I had around crowds.

"Hell if I know." Hanna burped. "Hey, Frank's throwing a party at his house. We should go."

"Yeah, sure," I mumbled. I got up and walked beyond the

edge of the shadows. Dozens of families were settling down on the grass in the middle of the park, eating and drinking. Some of the little ones were running around, chasing each other, screaming and giggling.

"There is something going on here today." I sat down next to Hanna, who was lying on the ground clearly uninterested in what was happening. I picked up a chocolate bar and broke it in half.

My attention kept drifting back toward the lawn with the steadily growing crowd. There must have been nearly fifty people now. The smell of barbequed meat wafted toward us. The smell reminded me of camping.

I studied my neon pink polished nails when suddenly the air around me seemed to vibrate. A large industrial vehicle drove onto the lawn. Four men got out and surveyed the park. One of the men pointed toward an empty space in the middle of the crowd. The other men pulled something out of the vehicle. The thing was partly covered with a sheet, but I immediately recognized the ivory and black keys. More people started to watch now, putting down their plates of food and standing still in complete bafflement.

"Hanna, you've got to see this! They've brought a piano," I said.

Hanna practically jumped up, and we watched the men lug this baby grand piano. I started clapping.


*Henryk Berlman*


He gazed at the sky as though he were looking for God. The cigarette in his hand burned halfway down before he realized he was still holding on to it.

"What are you thinking, Henryk?" Kasper inquired, rubbing his hands together because the air was crisp.

Henryk didn't answer immediately. He didn't like to have conversations before he performed. It wasn't superstition or that he was nervous. He just liked to keep to himself. His mind traveled thousands of miles away from the piano, from Warsaw, and even himself. The beauty of imagination and creation, he thought, was the chance to escape one reality and enter another.

"How many people do you think are here?" Henryk finally responded.

With his feet firmly planted in the grass, Kasper twisted his torso to survey the families eating and playing and the musicians and artists carrying their violins, cellos, guitars, and yes, even pianos.

"There must be at least two hundred now. I see five pianos already. When are you going to start playing?"

Henryk nodded silently and moved toward the stool, always keeping one hand touching the piano. When he sat down, he rested his fingers on the keys. The smooth, black and white surfaces felt cold. For a moment he closed his eyes, allowing himself to separate Henryk the music student from Henryk the pianist. When he opened his eyes, his slight frame seemed to expand and bloom as his arms floated over the keys. His fingers danced to the rhapsody inside his mind. The park, the crowd, and even his brother, Kasper, seemed to evaporate. He was alone with the music.

A small girl in crisp, blond braids ran up to the piano player. She kept her distance, but her eyes widened and her lips parted. A woman gathered the girl in her arms and balanced her on a hip so they could both watch.

"What's wrong with his eyes?" the girl asked.

"He's blind. But look how beautifully he plays Chopin."

## *The Jaworski Family*

"Come here, Hans," Mrs. Jaworski said, smoothing the picnic blanket to set up lunch for her two children and husband.

The small child, who could not have been more than five years old, ran even further from his parents, toward the other children. Mrs. Jaworski sighed, rubbing her temples with her fingers to ease the headache. Her husband, Gabriel, rubbed her back affectionately, laughing at his wild son. The other child was too young to even walk, and he sat on the grass, stretching his chubby limbs outward.

"Relax, Lena. Everyone is just having a good time. Look at that white piano. Isn't it beautiful?"

She nodded, gazing at the sea of pianos. There were twenty sporadically positioned throughout the entire park. She closed her eyes to listen to the waves of music emanating from these instruments. She opened her eyes and turned her head to look at the bronze statue of Chopin, his face gazing at all the people who had gathered here today to honor his legacy.

"It's amazing how many people love Chopin," Lena said.

"In a way, it's like Chopin is still alive. His compositions are his children."

Gabriel got up and ran toward his son. His movements were graceful, practically matching the rhythm of the music, Lena thought. His strides were long and his arms moved swiftly at his sides propelling him forward. Though Gabriel had retired from the ballet company years ago, his body was still strong and lean. He threw his son in the air, high above his head just as the music hit a crescendo.

When Lena had first met Gabriel, he was performing on the stage to a composition by Chopin. He seemed to fly across the floor. His slender legs were exposed, the overdeveloped muscles thinly covered with pale flesh.

Lena stood up suddenly. The wind picked up, pressing the thin material of her skirt against her legs, outlining them completely, and blowing her blond locks in all directions. The dozens of pianists hovered over their pianos, scattered all through the field, their bodies harnessed to the momentum of their playing. Each was in their own space in the music, oblivious to everything around them. She hardly listened to Chopin or classical music these days, but every time she heard Chopin, emotions stirred within her. She believed it was passion, love. A smile erupted on her lips as Gabriel and Hans ran back to her.

### *Justina*

From far away you would not have seen the teenager's thin frame pressed against the ground. Justina turned her head to one side, spreading her arms out, so that she looked like the letter "T." The cool blades of grass tickled her chin, but she resisted the temptation to move.

"What are you doing, Justina?" One of the girls in her group asked.

"The vibrations. I think I can feel them, ever so slightly."

There was a pause in the music. Justina sat up. Her white cotton dress was dotted with grass stains. A man began talking, his voice booming from the microphone. Justina stretched her frame to see, but the rows of people blocked her view of the speaker. She noticed people turning toward the statue.

"The occupying Germans destroyed the original statue in 1940. They wanted to weaken our resolve, the morale. They wanted to decimate everything that made us proud of Poland.

But no matter what they burned or destroyed, they couldn't reach what was inside our hearts. The flower may die, but the shadow still remains. Today we celebrate our love for Chopin and his music."

Applause and cheering erupted all around Justina. The momentum of the music started to build again, reaching a crescendo as the cheering subsided. She stood up, looking all around her. Pianos, dozens of them in all colors and sizes, covered the grounds. The majestic instruments reminded her of ships in the sea. Everyone was playing together harmoniously. Until tonight, Justina never thought much about Chopin or his music. She never played an instrument in her life. Yet now she was sure that she loved Chopin too.

"Hey! Come on." Someone tapped her on the shoulder. A group of boys and girls were running through the crowd.

She ran after them, jumping over picnic baskets, twisting her body to squeeze through clusters of people. The music from the pianos blended together into one harmonious force. Justina could feel the sound enveloping her, wave by wave. She ran faster, pumping her arms by her side, moving at the speed of sound. If there were a cosmic energy, the musicians and their audience could feel it. The weight of sound echoed to the heavens.

## RUMORS AND SECRETS

The whole time my father, Ira, spoke to me, I kept glancing at his long, arthritic fingers resting on the table. I wondered how long he had those amoeba-shaped liver spots on his hands. When I looked back at his face, he seemed more vulnerable to me. Or perhaps it was me. I felt more vulnerable watching my father get old.

"Margot, there is something I need to tell you," my father finally admitted.

"I already know." I sighed.

Everyone in the family knew.

As a child, when my mother used to tuck me in at night, I'd wait several minutes before crawling out of bed and sneaking out of the room. At the top of the staircase, I hid beneath a long, skinny, wood table with my Toni doll named Vicky. The two of us, with our faces pressed against the balusters, watched my mother talk to her mother, Grandma Vivien, about my father. These were the days when my father drove a taxi on weeknights in New York City.

"But why would they wait until he was a grown man to tell him?" Vivien asked.

My mother sighed. "It was a real scandal. His father got his cousin pregnant. She was only seventeen. He was thirty-two. I think that's what I heard." My mother tapped her lip with her index finger.

"I'm surprised that Ira's father would allow himself to be caught in such a situation. He seemed to me to be so . . . aloof," my grandmother said.

"He married Evelyn when Ira was only two," my mother explained, lighting a cigarette. "She treated Ira like he was her own, so they felt there was no need to tell him the truth. It was different back then. You should understand."

My grandmother nodded, taking several slow sips from her tea. She was facing away from me, but I could still imagine her steely, ice blue eyes narrowing. She did this a lot when she and my mother gossiped about the family.

"I always thought there was something a little odd about that family," Vivien said. "So his father was never going to tell him?"

My mother shook her head. "When Ira joined the army in 1943, a lawyer and his mother and father sat him down and said, 'Ira, your family needs to tell you something before you go off to war. Ira is not your real name. It's Alexander, and Evelyn Schwartz is not your birth mother. Your natural mother died in childbirth.'"

My mother leaned forward toward Vivien, lowering her voice. "I found a photo of her in his sock drawer. Margot looks so much like her with the fiery red hair and milky skin."

I was so fascinated that I leaned forward. The doll's face slipped through the balusters, and her body plummeted, landing face down on the couch between my mother and grandmother. They stared at the doll for a long, uncomfortable moment before glancing up toward the staircase. My clammy hands gripped the balusters harder.

My mother recovered from the surprise, and instead of looking angry, she patted her lap.

"Come here, sweetie. It's okay." Her voice had a warm tone, but I still took my time coming down the stairs.

She wrapped her arms around me, pulling me onto her lap. Her bony knees dug into the back of my calves.

She spoke softly and slowly. "You can't talk about what you just heard to your father. It would make him very upset. Do you understand? You can't say anything." My mother twisted my face toward hers so that our eyes were only inches away from each other.

I didn't understand, but something about the way my mother's eyes scrutinized my face prevented me from asking any questions.

Now, as an adult, I could see the weight of this secret rest heavily on my father's rounded shoulders.

"Why didn't you tell me you knew?" My father asked. He looked more hurt than surprised.

"I figured you would talk to me about it when you were ready," I lied. I always had a feeling he might never want to talk about the loss of his biological mother.

Leaning back in the booth, my father let out a long sigh. He waited for the waitress to remove our plates before he spoke.

"My family was terrified of death, and instead of talking about it, we tried to forget the dead. But it's impossible to forget," he said. "And the story itself . . . I don't think anyone wanted to acknowledge what happened."

"What was your mother's name?" I asked.

"Galina. I don't know much about her. My father never brought her up when I was around. I do know that she had very thick, curly, red hair. Like you."

"Why didn't you ask your father about her?"

He looked confused, and I worried that I had trespassed a certain line that I shouldn't have crossed. He clasped his hands together, looking off into the distance thinking for a moment.

"You know, I just never thought to ask. I never questioned subject matters that were off limits. In hindsight I wish that I did."

I nodded, trying to disguise my disappointment. I wanted Galina to be more than a scandalous rumor, an elusive figure, a wallet-sized photo stuffed in a sock drawer. But my father never spoke of her again. I knew my father would never forget his mother, but in the end, he remained faithful to his fears, relegating this young woman to the shadows of memories long repressed.

## CLOUDBURST

"Happy birthday, Tes. Congratulations on making twenty-one rotations around the sun." Aubrey grabbed a mason jar filled with vodka and cranberry juice and handed it to Tesla. "Sorry. I know you prefer tequila, but this was the closest we could get."

A laugh escaped from Tesla that wasn't fully genuine, but an honest attempt to be in a cheery mood. "Thanks. I'm just grateful that I get to be with good friends. However, I do appreciate *this*. Cheers." Tesla held up her mason jar while Aubrey and her on-again, off-again boyfriend, Aiden, raised their mugs. Tesla purposely took a large gulp and relished the burning sensation traveling down her throat into her stomach. The subtle numbness through her body was a welcomed sensation to her. "It'll be five months tomorrow."

Some nights Tesla, along with Aubrey and Aiden, would climb up on the roof of Aubrey's house and gaze at the trailblazing sunset. At first it was to see what was going on in the neighborhood, but after a while, they sat on the roof just to find some escape from their reality.

"Sometimes I feel like it happened yesterday, and other times it feels like it's always been this way," Aiden said.

Tesla understood how Aiden felt. She remembered the day so clearly. It was Friday, October 22nd. Her mother was supposed fly in from New York late that night. Tesla and Aubrey had decided to have dinner and catch a movie before Tesla went to pick up her mother from the airport. It was while they were sitting in the theater forty-five minutes into the movie that everything went dark. At first, no one moved or said a word. A voice came through the loud speaker announcing there was a massive power outage and all patrons would be compensated with a free popcorn and large-size drink.

"Lame!" A man said two rows back from where Aubrey and Tesla sat.

The auditorium was glowing now with the flashlights from people's cell phones. Many were already leaving, grumbling about the movie being cut short. Aubrey and Tesla trailed behind the crowd, which was steadily getting larger as all the auditoriums began to empty.

When they reached Tesla's car, Aubrey suggested they go to the airport together to pick up her mother. The drive was slow and long. Without the traffic lights, every intersection became a chaotic four-way stop. Fortunately, the traffic wasn't heavy, but the drivers were noticeably aggravated and unnerved by the situation, which Tesla and Aubrey realized was affecting the entire metropolitan area of Phoenix. The freeway was much calmer, and for a brief moment, Tesla felt more at ease.

"Wow! That's creepy. I've never seen the airport look like that." Aubrey nodded toward Sky Harbor International Airport, which was barely visible in the darkness without its usual yellow glow of outdoor lights.

"It's so quiet." Tesla turned on her phone's flashlight as they made the long walk from the furthest parking lot to the terminal. Aubrey hated the parking structures at the airport, and considering tonight's circumstances, Tesla wasn't going to argue with her.

"Yeah. Just wait until we get inside. It's going to be chaos. People are going to be *piiiisssssed*." Aubrey drawled the last word to two syllables.

The terminal was busy, but fortunately, not as chaotic as Aubrey anticipated. By now, travelers were already surrendering to the inconvenience. Many were sitting against the walls or on their luggage, using their forearms and handkerchiefs to wipe the sweat off their foreheads. The air felt warm and suffocating, and Tesla saw her anxiety reflected in the eyes of everyone around her. Tesla and Aubrey stood in line for almost an hour, waiting to talk to airport personnel.

"Ma'am, I'm sorry, but there's nothing I can do until the power comes back on. No planes leaving and no planes coming in. That's all I can tell you for now," the woman behind the ticket counter responded more than once.

"Hi," Tesla said nervously, because the woman's face was a severe scowl by this point. "I heard what you told the others, but my mother is flying in from New York. Her plane is supposed to land in less than an hour. Do you have *any* information on her flight?"

The woman sighed dramatically. "No, I don't have any information. They'll have to land at a different airport and, if the power comes back on soon, they'll continue here or they'll reschedule their flight."

"Right. Of course," Tesla answered, feeling sheepish now. She ran her hand over the back of her neck, which felt warm and sticky from sweat.

"Don't worry. This must've happened before." Aubrey put

her arm around Tesla's shoulders. "Your mom will text you as soon as they land. It's just annoying, but we'll laugh about it later."

But they never laughed about it later. The power never came back on. The first few days felt like a holiday to Tesla. Two days after the power went out, Tesla rode her bike to the restaurant where she worked just to see if she could find out what was happening. Tesla pushed the heavy oak door open. The smell of freshly cooked food hit Tesla so hard that she pressed her lips together. All she had eaten in the last two days were leftovers that were starting to go bad since her fridge was quickly becoming obsolete and her oven was electric. She hadn't realized how much she'd missed a cooked meal.

The restaurant was empty of patrons, but a couple of the cooks, waiters, and the owner were sitting around one of the large circular tables. Some of them were still eating eggs with potato fritters or chicken cutlets with baked potatoes.

"I thought you were taking the week off." Shannon was the first to notice Tesla standing in the corner. Shannon, a tall, broad-shouldered woman in her late thirties, was one of the waitresses who often had the same shift as Tesla.

"I was supposed to, but my mother's plane never made it here," Tesla said.

The owner of the restaurant, Manny, quickly turned in his seat. His usually stern expression showed genuine concern.

"Oh, I'm so sorry to hear that, sweetie. Did you try texting her?" He asked.

"Yeah, but it wouldn't go through. I tried like a hundred times," she said.

"Don't jump to any conclusions. Sometimes things look worse than they actually are." Manny stood up, wiping his tortoise shell glasses with his shirt. "Fortunately, the generator is working and Shannon got our gas range started, so I cooked up some food for everyone. There's plenty in the kitchen. Help yourself."

"Where you goin'?" Shannon asked Manny.

"I'm going to get the cash out of my office. I'm going to give each of you two hundred dollars. When you leave here, I want you to go and get yourself plenty of water and food. Some of the stores will take cash. Fill up your tanks if you can, and then lay low until you hear something."

"What do you mean? You just said not to jump to any conclusions." One of the cooks said.

"People might start to get a little crazy. Right now, people think it's a bad outage, but when they run out of cash or food or water—"

"People are going to be looting is what he means," Shannon interrupted. "People are going to start losing it."

Jesse, who was a couple years younger than Tesla, started picking up the empty plates to carry them back to the kitchen as though he were still working his shift. He stopped in front of the swinging door to the kitchen and faced the group. His full cheeks, which had usually reddened easily, looked unnaturally pale. "My uncle has a ham radio, and he said that the outage is at least nationwide. No one has any idea when the grid will be fixed."

Sensing people's anxiety rising, Manny interjected, "Look, none of us really knows what's going to happen. They could fix the power tomorrow. The point is there's nothing wrong with taking some precaution. I don't want any of you to get caught up in any unnecessary danger."

Tesla had never seen this side of Manny. Of course she rarely spoke to him because he was usually overseeing the construction of another restaurant he was opening. He was reserved but fair with his employees. Tesla guessed that he must be about the same age as her mother. After she helped herself to eggs and potato fritters, she took the money Manny handed to her and stuffed most of it inside her boot and headed to the nearest grocery store.

No one knew when the looting and outbreak of violence really began. Tesla holed herself up in her apartment, except when she was able to gather enough courage to go out for more supplies. Besides water, she made sure to stock up on nonperishables like peanut butter, protein bars, cereal, jerky, soup, and whatever else she could get easily and cheaply. At first it was just a few convenience stores that were ransacked. As the days passed, the destruction spread like a virus, hitting buildings randomly in different parts of the city. Security and the police heavily monitored some places, but there weren't enough officers to protect every building from the onslaught of desperate people.

Even though it was October, Phoenix was still hot during the afternoons. Tesla tried reading or cleaning to calm her nerves. When the warm stagnant air from the apartment tired her, she lay down on the floor and stared at the ceiling. Sometimes she caught herself reaching for her phone or flipping a light switch. There was always a mild, gnawing pain in her stomach, which she tried relieving with a cigarette. Her mother was a smoker and had left a pack in the pantry. Before now, Tesla only smoked occasionally, but now it was the only thing she could think to do to keep her thoughts at bay. At night, she sat on the balcony and watched for any activity. The street was quiet with the occasional car passing. She wondered where her mother was. Was she safe? Was she still alive? Today they were supposed to drive up to Sedona to hike the West Fork Trail and then shop in those New Age stores her mother liked so much.

Tesla was so wrapped up in her thoughts that the knock at her door caused her chest to tighten. It was Aubrey. She was wearing cutoffs and a tank shirt. Her red, curly hair was more frizzy than usual, and her hands had a slight tremor.

"I think you should come stay with me. I don't think either one of us should be alone right now," Aubrey blurted.

"Are you okay? Let me get you water." Tesla ran to the table, which was piled with packages of bottled water.

Aubrey dropped onto the couch; her pale blue eyes stared at the ceiling. "People are crazy, Tes. I just saw a woman in a wheelchair get the crap kicked out of her because they were fighting over water. No one carries cash anymore, so now people are just grabbing whatever they can and they don't care who's in their way. Then this guy shoved me so hard that I fell because he couldn't wait two seconds for me to get out of his way. You know what he was in a rush for? Potato chips! That junk makes you even thirstier! It's only been four days, Tes, and sanity has gone completely out the window."

Tesla thought about Manny and the money he gave her. She was sure there weren't too many bosses who showed that much care toward their employees.

"There are good people out there. They're just needles in the haystack, but they're out there." Tesla sighed heavily as she plopped down next to Aubrey.

"I feel both stupid and useless." Aubrey pulled out her cell-phone from her back pocket. "I'm going through withdrawal. My access to the world came from this phone and now it's just a flashlight."

"I wish I knew my mom was safe," Tesla said.

"I know. She's okay. We have to believe that." Aubrey patted Tesla's knee and glanced toward the kitchen table, which was stacked with water, peanut butter, bread, a few canned goods, and snacks. "You don't mess around, do you?"

"I had to go to ten different places. They wouldn't let us take more than one case of water. It's going to get worse.

We've watched enough postapocalyptic movies to know how this is going to go." Tesla sat up and peeled her sweat-dampened shirt from her back.

"Do you really think this is it?"

Tesla shrugged her shoulders. "Who knows? I hope not."

## April

It was Tesla's turn to forage for supplies. She waited until the sky had just started to lighten at the edges of the horizon. Tesla had found that there were fewer people out foraging early in the morning, which meant less trouble, as far as she was concerned. She went to a different neighborhood every time, just in case someone saw her. She wanted to be invisible. Standing in the crisp morning air, Tesla shivered, gripping the straps of her backpack. In the five months since the power outage, an increasing number of people had left the city, probably to head north, Tesla figured. She would never get used to the abandoned houses rapidly deteriorating from neglect. A feeling of nostalgia passed through her. She remembered sitting in the backseat of her mother's Honda Accord looking at these homes, which, though they were plain, were maintained and had families living inside them. Now these homes, broken, abandoned, and forgotten, were a reminder of how far they had declined and how quickly.

She walked briskly, sweeping her gaze back and forth to make sure she was alone. Yet the silence unsettled her, too. She didn't really want to be alone, but she did want to survive. Suddenly a dog's deep, barking growl pierced the stillness. Tesla jumped and involuntarily covered her mouth with her hand. She had trained herself not to scream. None of the houses looked particularly safe, but she ran toward the one closest to her. From the outside, the house looked like all the others: small, three-bedroom homes made out of block with carports instead of garages. All of the front windows were either cracked or shattered. The door was ajar, but not broken. Glass crunched beneath her worn combat boots as she slowly made her way through the kitchen. In the living room, she saw urine stains against the walls, and she instinctively held her breath and covered her nose and mouth. There wasn't much food left, but Tesla found two cans of tomato soup, five packets of oatmeal, and thirteen mini packets of ketchup. She knew this wasn't enough, but she wasn't ready to leave.

There was something about this house that felt different to her. Every house she went to still had a little of its character left. The looters always took valuables, food, and weapons, if there were any, but they didn't usually raid for trinkets and photographs. Tesla always took a moment to look at the family portraits or personal items that were left behind. There were no family photographs in this house. Tesla slowly walked through all the rooms, keeping a mental inventory of every-thing she saw. The rack of men's shirts and pants hanging in the master bedroom closet told her a little something about the owner. He wore size twelve dark brown Doc Martens. From the size of his clothes, he must have been about six feet tall and fairly slender. She moved on to the next bedroom, which looked like his office. This room was darker than the others. Thick, tan-colored curtains blocked out all the sunlight. Against her better judgment, she walked into the room before turning on her flashlight. Feeling a sharp pain in her shin, Tesla fell backward into the closet door. She hobbled to the window to open the curtains, and she sat down to hug her throbbing leg. While all the other rooms were sparse, this space had more character. The desk, which was lying on its side, had a steampunk design and was made of wood and copper. She also noticed against the opposite wall, several collectible action figures that had fallen off the shelf. The rest of the room was buried with papers, comic books, magazines, and food wrappers.

There was a keyboard, remarkably still sitting on its stand, and two framed posters of *Star Wars: Return of the Jedi* and a black-and-white drawn portrait of a photographer named Robert Capa. The blood seeped through her fingers, and she grabbed a handkerchief from her backpack and wrapped her leg with it. She got mad at herself for being careless. She then saw the culprit of her wound, a broken lamp that had the Captain America emblem printed on the base. She kicked it out of her way, and that's when she saw an envelope, the corner of it peeking through the mess. Tesla reached for the envelope. "The Twelve Shots" was scrawled across the sealed manila envelope. She tore it open. Several 8x10 photos slipped out onto the floor. Her fingers gently spread the photos on the floor.

The front door suddenly crashed open. Tesla's heart raced. These days people felt like they had nothing left to lose. She knew that if they found her they could kill her. She stuffed the photos into her backpack. There was no time to escape through the window, so she took cover behind the desk. She heard two distinct male voices. The words became clearer as they walked down the hallway toward the two bedrooms. It took all her strength not to run out of the house screaming. The terror she felt was painful, both physically and mentally. When so many days felt like this, she wondered why she didn't become more used to it.

"Dude, this place's been stripped." The man's voice was deep and sounded aggressive.

Tesla imagined his face ugly and angry looking, his body thick and reeking of sweat. Focus, she thought angrily to herself, don't let your thoughts drift there.

"It doesn't look like there was much here to begin with."
This other voice was higher and less rough.

She heard a pair of footsteps belonging to the second voice
walk into the office. He dropped onto one knee and pulled a
box that was just inches from her head behind the desk.

"Jordan! Look at this. I woulda killed for this game a year
ago." A sinewy, pale arm waved a video game box in the air.

"Just looking at that crap makes me depressed," the other
moaned. "Come on. I'm not gonna sit here and go through this
crap so you can walk down memory lane. I'm hungry, and I ran
out of cigarettes three days ago. You don't want to test my
patience right now, bud."

"Fine. Whatever. I'm using the john first, though."

Tesla rolled her eyes. The suspense was going to kill her
before she even had a chance to escape.

"I bet it's already trashed. Let's go," Jordan bellowed.

Against the wishes of both Tesla and Jordan, the game-
driven guy went into the master bedroom to use the toilet.
Jordan went out to the backyard to wait. After what felt like
several agonizing minutes, the two men left. Very quietly, Tesla
pulled the curtains back and managed to push the window
open. As soon as her boots touched the gravel, she sprinted.
The adrenaline pumping inside her made her forget about the
pain in her leg and the burning in her chest.

An hour later, Tesla was in her corner of the room, which
was the computer room in Aubrey's house. She had a fresh
bandage on her leg. She spread the photos she had found
across her makeshift bed of two sleeping bags and a comforter.
There were twelve pictures in total. At first glance she really
didn't see any correlation between the images. In fact, they
appeared random.

"What are you doing here, Tes? You didn't find enough.
We're going to starve if we don't find something in the next

couple of days. We're short enough as it is." Aiden leaned against the doorframe, crossing his arms against his chest as though he were her parent.

"I'm sorry. It's getting harder to find places that haven't been picked off yet."

"I know. We'll just have to try harder –" He looked down, and suddenly his stern mood lifted. "Hey! What's that?" He sat down next to her and picked up a photo with a woman, dressed in a black patent latex dress so short her bottom was exposed. She was dancing, her back facing a group of men.

"Wow." Aiden's bushy dark brows shot upward. "I didn't know this was your thing."

"Surprise. Cat's out of the bag now." Tesla rolled her eyes at Aiden and continued sorting through the photos. Each one was of a completely different subject matter so that the photos didn't seem to belong in a group. "I just don't get it. I don't see a theme. It's so disjointed."

Aiden held the photo of the woman and then he picked up another one, which showed a homeless man wrapped in a dirty blanket. He was mostly hidden by pedestrians walking in front of him, completely oblivious to his pathetic presence.

"I found these at a house this morning. There was something about these photos that I couldn't let go. But I don't really understand what I'm looking at," Tesla said.

"Maybe this photographer just liked taking random pictures," he said. "I mean, how are these two even related?"

"I don't know," Tesla said softly, "but there's a reason why he called them 'The Twelve Shots,' so there has to be a connection."

"What's the point?"

She shrugged. "I'm not sure. What else do we have to do, anyways?"

Tesla stared at the photographs as though they were pieces

to a puzzle. She felt as though she were meant to discover these pictures. However, she couldn't even find a common theme. Besides the snapshots of the scantily clad woman and homeless man, there was a photograph of a line of fully self-checkout machines in the grocery store. Everything was white, glossy, and sleek. Lines of customers, holding and pushing red plastic shopping carts filled to the brim with food, were scanning and bagging their own purchases.

Another image was a wide shot of a crowded coffee shop. Every table was occupied. The patrons, who sipped coffee from large, white porcelain mugs, were either working on laptops or gazing at their cell phones. Tesla sighed. There wasn't anything unusual about this photo or any of them, for that matter.

The next image was a school playground with a group of children, around the age of ten. Two girls were on the swing set, but their faces were looking off to the side where there were four boys standing just next to the swings. Tesla looked more closely and saw that one of the boys was holding his face in his hands as if he were crying. His pants were stained with mud. Three other boys stood laughing and pointing at the distraught boy. Tesla felt a pang in her chest for the boy.

The next photograph completely confused Tesla. She knew right away that it was a picture of the sky. There were four thick, white trails crossing the sky, but she didn't understand why someone would bother taking such a photograph. She was getting tired and hungry. She put the photographs back into the envelope and lay down, putting her arms behind her head. Her leg was throbbing, but she felt too exhausted to get up and look for aspirin. After a few minutes, she grabbed the envelope again.

She pulled out a photograph of an old, abandoned strip

mall. The windows were either shattered or boarded. Another shot showed two slender young women taking a selfie in front of a fountain. They wore midriff-baring halter tops and micro-minis. Their young faces were perfectly contoured, their eyelids sparkled with metallic eye shadow, and their nails glittered with long, fake, stiletto nails. Both girls looked completely happy, like they were having the best time. Tesla could remember wanting to look more like those girls, but she never had the confidence to wear those clothes, and the art of makeup escaped her.

Aubrey walked in the room and lay down next to Tesla, turning her head to look at the photos. "Don't worry about today and Aiden. I know we're all doing our best. By the way, what are we looking at?"

"I don't know. I think there's something here, but I can't figure it out. I mean, these images, though some are kind of disturbing, they seem like normal, everyday life to me."

Aubrey picked up the photo of the two girls. "They remind me of my freshman year at college. Class was like intermission between the parties," Aubrey quipped.

Tesla smiled. She pulled out another photo from the envelope and held it in front of them. A bride and groom were taking their vows, but what caught Tesla's attention were the rows of camera phones held in the air as friends and family members recorded the ceremony.

"You see it all the time. I hate when people record concerts. They completely miss the point of going to a show," Aubrey said.

"*We* did that too. Documenting our lives. . ." Tesla selected another two images to examine. One of the photos showed a billboard for a weight loss clinic right next to a fast food restaurant. The other photo showed a large body of water that was heavily littered with trash. The photographer had zoomed in on the water as though to make the objects in the water seem even bigger.

"Look at this one," Aubrey said, grabbing a third photo and tapping Tesla's arm. "I've heard stories about road rage like this."

Tesla took the photo from Aubrey. She wasn't sure how the photographer managed to get this shot because it seemed as though he were only a few feet away from the conflict. Two cars were stopped in the midst of a busy street. A woman was pulling another woman out of the driver's seat by her hair. When Tesla looked really closely at the second car, she thought she could see a child sitting helplessly in the passenger seat.

"This is disturbing." Tesla shuddered and put the photos back in the envelope. She had looked at all of them now, and she didn't feel like she had gained any more clarity on the meaning of these pictures. "I want to go back there and see if I missed something," Tesla said.

"Is it really worth it?" Aubrey sat up. "We kind of have bigger problems here. These photos aren't going to help us. It's the past. This is now, and it looks nothing like these photos."

"Look. Don't worry. I'll go out again to look for more food. We'll get by," Tesla reassured Aubrey. In her heart, Tesla knew she had to return to the house where she found the photographs.

"Don't leave now. It's really dangerous." Aubrey reached for Tesla's elbow. "I'm serious. My neighbor was telling me there's a group that's breaking into homes and slaughtering anyone who gets in their way."

"I'll wait until tomorrow morning. I'll leave super early. No one is doing much at that time."

* * *

A few days passed before Tesla gathered the nerve to go back to the house. Her last experience there was the closest she had ever been to danger. She felt that she was tempting fate by going back. The night before she slept only a few hours. Just as the sky started to lighten on the horizon, Tesla got dressed and left quietly on her bike. The empty streets and silence comforted her. It was one of the few moments in the past six months where she felt peace. During the ride, she didn't think about where she would get more water or food because she couldn't carry the fear anymore. She needed a break.

When she reached the house, she carried the bike into the house and propped it against the wall in the kitchen. She was careful to listen for any sound and make certain that the house was empty. The office looked the same as when she was last here, but of course, it was so messy before that she wasn't sure she would even know if someone had moved anything. She rapidly rummaged through the piles, but she couldn't find anything relating to the photos. Frustration and anger overwhelmed her, and she ran the back of her hand under her eyes.

"Who are you?"

Tesla whirled around toward the door. A heavily bearded man wearing a dark blue flannel shirt and cargo pants stood there. An expression of anger and confusion was more than apparent on his face. Tesla instinctively reached for her knife tucked in her combat boot.

"Whoa! Hold on there!" The man held up both hands in a gesture of surrender. "I'm just looking for the guy who lives here. Put that knife down."

"You know who lived here?" She asked needlessly.

"He's my brother, Robert. My name is Andrew. Who are you?"

"Tesla."

"Oh, like the inventor."

"Well, I was technically named after the band, which was probably named after the inventor. So, yeah, I guess." She tucked the knife back in her boot and handed the envelope to Andrew. "I found these a few days ago, and I was trying to figure out what they meant. I was hoping I would find some explanation."

Andrew shuffled through the photos quickly. His face looked nonchalant or indifferent. Tesla couldn't tell, but she was beginning to fear that maybe she really had wasted her time.

"Do you know what these pictures mean?" Andrew asked.

Tesla shook her head, "It just looks like life to me."

"As you know it," Andrew interjected.

"But I still don't get it," she said.

"My brother and I are a lot older than you, so we know that life didn't always look like this. My brother saw the changes. I don't think he was trying to judge. He's not that kind of person. His photography was more about showing people how he saw the world." Andrew handed the envelope back to Tesla. "I think these were meant for you."

"Where do you think your brother went?" Tesla asked.

"Knowing my brother, he's probably trying to document this drastic time. He could be anywhere. I was in Michigan when it happened, and I slowly made my way down here. No one really knows what's going on. I just wish I could find Robert."

Tesla let herself fall against the wall. It was the first time the anxiety of surviving was replaced with a heaviness that wrapped around her chest. She could see the expanse of her life in this apocalyptic wasteland. Andrew pulled out a pack of cigarettes and the two of them went outside on the back porch and sat on two rusting folding chairs.

"Was Robert a photojournalist?" Tesla asked.

"He did some freelance work, but he made his living photographing products for a jewelry store," Andrew answered.

"Thank you for letting me keep these photos. I'll do my best to protect them." Tesla held the cigarette in front of her as though she were studying it. "You know, these go for a lot these days."

"Sometimes it's the simple pleasures that get you through some really dark times."

"We're not going to survive the summer here. We'll die from the heat."

"Don't say that," Andrew interrupted. "You can't think too far ahead. One day at a time."

There was silence between them, though it didn't feel awkward. They both stared out at the backyard, which was small and sparsely landscaped with two dying orange trees and a pine tree. Tesla felt a sense of serenity in that moment, even though the lawn was overgrown with weeds and most of the potted plants were fried. The backyard was the only part of the property that wasn't vandalized. Sometimes she was able to forget about the reality of her situation, even if it was only for a few minutes. Her mind wandered into the past, when her biggest problem was having the Friday night shift at the restaurant when she would have rather gone out with her friends.

"Take this," Andrew handed Tesla a maroon-colored keychain in the shape of Arizona with the Arizona State University Sun Devil logo. "My Aunt Carol lives in Cornville. She's a little rough around the edges, but she's lived off the land, and she's probably handling her own okay. It's up north. Take I-17 to McGuireville and just keep following the road until you see The Grasshopper Grill. Make a left. It's a dark blue house with three big pine trees. Show her this key chain. She'll know it's mine."

Tesla repeated the information to him until he was sure she had memorized it.

"Why are you helping me?" she asked.

"I have a feeling you're a good person." Andrew walked back toward the sliding doors that led into the kitchen. He turned around and smiled gently. "Besides, I gave you my brother's photos."

When Tesla returned from the house, she noticed Aubrey looked pale and shaken.

"Aiden's been out for hours. He's never been gone this long. I think there's something wrong," Aubrey said.

Tesla told her about Aunt Carol.

"We finally have a place where we can go. Let's pack what we need, so when Aiden gets back, we can leave," Tesla suggested.

They packed only their essentials in their backpacks in the event they had to leave the car behind at some point. Tesla made sure Robert's photographs were tucked safely inside her backpack.

By that evening Aiden still hadn't returned and Aubrey paced, "Should we go out and find him? We should take your car because it's got more gas. We can look for him and then head north. I think I know where he was going this morning." Aubrey was speaking quickly.

Tesla hugged Aubrey. "We can't go out looking for him. We wouldn't stand a chance. We'll wait a little longer." Tesla and Aubrey sat on the couch sharing a cigarette and the last beer, while they waited for Aiden.

"I'm going to miss this house. It's the first time I've lived anywhere longer than five years," Aubrey said so softly, Tesla leaned forward instinctively.

"I'm sorry we have to leave, too. Phoenix has always been my home."

Two hours later Aubrey and Tesla sat huddled together, their faces drawn with worry and fear. Aiden never returned.

Tesla squeezed Aubrey's hand. "We should really get going."

Aubrey started to cry as she gathered her things. "I feel bad leaving—"

Two loud pops shattered the otherwise quiet evening. Aubrey and Tesla jumped up and ran toward the window that overlooked the front yard. Aubrey parted the curtains. The last of the sun's rays illuminated a man standing on the front lawn of her neighbor's house across the street. He was waving a gun in the air and shouting something that Tesla couldn't hear clearly. There was a group of men and women, their faces distorted with rage and hunger. They were all yelling and sneering. Then one of them turned around and noticed Tesla and Aubrey.

"They saw us. We gotta leave now!" Tesla pushed a bookcase in front of the door.

They raced through the kitchen toward the backyard. Tesla could already hear the windows giving way to the threatening crowd. She heard Aubrey scream. The front door burst open as they bolted into the backyard. There was so much shouting and, with what sounded like gunfire, Tesla lost track of Aubrey's screams. Her own panic drowned the shouting of violence behind her, and she escaped out into the darkening night.

# HUMAN CANNONBALL

Before Dickie's body was found floating in Lake Pleasant, it used to be just the three of us: me, Levi, and Dickie. Levi and Dickie were twins. Dickie was scrawnier than Levi and always the target for some bully. His loud mouth didn't help, either. He never held back. I tried to look out for him because I could be the most confrontational and aggressive in the group. Dickie didn't have a filter, and neither did I. We did whatever felt right to us at that moment. Maybe that's why I felt closer with him than with other people.

The last time we spoke, we were outside a mall in Phoenix finishing the last of our lunch and waiting for things to quiet down in the parking lot. We were taking care of a job for Cam, who ran a car theft business on the side. Dickie and I kept this from Levi. He wouldn't have agreed or understood, but Dickie and I were all right with that.

The temperature had already reached over a hundred degrees, and I started to feel impatient. The back of my shirt was already soaked with sweat and sticking to my skin. I pulled out some dice that I had stolen from another car and began rolling them on the pavement. I usually had a rule against keeping anything from the cars we stole, but for some reason I couldn't part with the dice.

Dickie and I were scanning the parking lot. A guy about our age waddled out of the mall. His pants were pulled down so low that his bright red boxers were exposed.

"Hey, Logan," Dickie said to me, nodding toward the guy with the red shorts. "I see Christmas."

"Don't," I started to say, but Dickie was already standing up. "We don't need the attention."

Naturally, Dickie didn't listen to me. He caught up to the guy as he reached the curb. Before he even had a chance to turn around, Dickie yanked his pants down to his ankles and pushed him over. He was still lying on his back when Dickie walked back and sat back down. The guy pulled his pants back up (higher this time) and probably considered coming for Dickie. I didn't move or say a word. He sized up the two of us and decided to let it go.

The parking lot was beginning to quiet down. I got up and started walking toward the rows of cars.

"One of Cam's buddies sold his guitar pedals to me for dirt cheap," Dickie said. "He bought all this gear thinking he was going to be some rock star. He was too lazy to learn. He hadn't even taken off the tags. I told him I'd take it all for eighty dollars. I was kidding, but he was like 'Sure. Take it.'"

Dickie took a long drag on his cigarette and smiled broadly as the smoke poured from his ruined mouth. Half of his teeth were missing; the result of him mouthing off to a guy who was bigger and faster. I was angry with him for not ever having the good sense to keep his mouth shut. At least I knew when to stay quiet.

"Now you and Levi can start jamming," I said.

"No way, man. I don't think Levi would go for that. Cam offered to jam with me sometime. He has a sweet drum kit."

"You know he's just cool with us because we earn money for him," I said.

"Nah. Cam's a cool guy. I'm not worried."

But I was worried. Dickie looked like he hadn't eaten anything in days, probably because of the pain in his mouth. The last fight took a toll on him. With his shaved head and sunken face, he seemed like a different person to me than the one I had always known.

"Cam wants us to go to that new development tomorrow. He says that the people there are always leaving their garage doors open," Dickie said, his eyes lighting up from the adrenaline rush.

"That's stupid," I said, pausing to admire a brand new Hyundai Tiburon. "Cam's not smart enough to make this operation any bigger. If we take on any more, it will be just a matter of time before one of us gets caught."

"What about that one?" Dickie nodded at a newer cobalt blue Ford F150.

I shook my head. "Too new. We need something older."

"Aww, man. Cam needs to update his shop so we can start getting into the newer models. That truck is sweet." Dickie adjusted his beanie. "Cam found a '73 Chevelle at the junk yard. It's just a shell, but he said if I got it fixed up, I could take it. I'm sure some of the guys at his shop could help me out."

"We'll see. I'd rather have a Honda del Sol."

"Dude, we steal more Hondas than anything else," Dickie retorted. Sometimes he thought he was smarter than he really was.

I shrugged. "I know, but I still like them."

We maintained a slow, steady pace as we moved through the parking lot. I kept my gaze on the few people coming and going from the mall. So far, everything was to our advantage, and I wanted to keep it that way.

"That one," I said and nodded at a dark red Ford Explorer. The SUV wasn't in perfect shape; splotches of faded paint covered the hood and roof. I stuck my fingernail between the seal and the window. Dickie handed me a Slim Jim and moved toward the front of the car, waiting for me to pop the hood. As soon as I got the door opened, I hopped into the driver seat. The heat from the vinyl burned through my pants. The owner was a smoker. The mixture of cigarette butts and a pine scented freshener hanging from the rearview mirror was strong.

My hands started shaking when I cracked the steering column. This had never happened to me. Usually these moments were the only time my mind worked smoothly, when all the garbage in my head disappeared. I looked out the window, but no one was nearby.

"How much longer?" Dickie called, slamming the hood shut. He slid into the passenger seat, wiping the sweat on his face with his sleeve. "Dude, what's your problem?"

"Almost got it," I answered.

I clenched the screwdriver, smashing it into the lock mechanism. The sound of crunching metal was always the worst part for me. It made me feel exposed. The probability for success depended on me doing this right and as fast as possible. I twisted the screwdriver with force this time. My palms were moist with sweat and the plastic holder slid in my grip.

Dickie swiveled in his seat, pulling his legs underneath him, "Speed it up. We've got someone walking in this direction. He's about fifteen cars away."

I wiped my hands on my shirt and took hold of the screwdriver again.

"Logan!" Dickie yelled.

"Damn it," I shouted, throwing my entire body into it this time. The screwdriver turned, and the accessory light lit up. Radiohead blasted through the speakers. I fumbled through all the knobs until I found the right one.

"It's too late," Dickie gasped.

"Shh!"

"Logan, we gotta get out of here now. We can't let him see us." Dickie twisted in his seat to look out the back window.

" . . . hey, what are you doing? HEY!" A heavyset man dropped his bags and was barreling toward the car, shaking his fist in the air. "Get out of my car! I'm gonna beat the shit out of you!"

"Aww, man. We were too slow–" Dickie groaned.

"Damn it, Dickie. Shut up already."

The spot in front of me was empty. I pressed hard on the gas pedal, and the car lurched through the space. I jerked on the steering wheel, maneuvering through the narrow rows between parked vehicles until I saw an exit. Some girl was taking her sweet time crossing the intersection, and I honked, edging the car closer to her. She got the point and ran to the other side. I slipped into traffic, nestling between a bus and a larger SUV. Dividing my attention between the car in front of me and the rear-view mirror, I cranked up the AC and pointed all the vents toward me. My skin felt like it was burning off my face.

Dickie leaned back in his seat and pulled out a cigarette.

"Sure. Just make yourself at home," I said and turned off the air and rolled down both front windows.

"Are you all right?" Dickie asked.

"No. Of course I'm not okay," I said with a little more hostility than I meant to. "This could've wrecked our lives."

"No, man. We're all right. He didn't get a good look at us."

"The point is, we almost got caught. Don't you get it? This is serious," I said.

"Just chill, dude. What's your problem? You've been angry all day," Dickie accused.

"I didn't mind when we were just hanging out and doing this every now and again for some extra money. But now Cam wants us doing this a lot, like this is all we do." I took a cigarette from Dickie's pack.

"Yeah, well, not all of us have a *real* job," Dickie said.

My heart was still racing. I had never come this close to being caught. "I make ten dollars an hour trimming people's backyards, and I still live at home. It's not like I have it much better than you. At least your brother lets you crash at his place for free. Cam treats us all right as long as we're doing whatever he says, but he'd screw us over the first chance he got."

The traffic was light, but I kept the speed at the limit so we wouldn't attract any attention. I avoided the freeways and took surface streets. My heart finally stopped racing. I looked over at Dickie, who seemed even more pathetic to me.

"What are they gonna do about your teeth?" I asked.

"Nothing. Access says they'll just yank the rest of the ones in my mouth and give me falsies. No thanks. I'll just keep the ones I got."

"Does it hurt?"

"It's okay. I just can't drink anything cold or the sockets start to ache real bad."

When we arrived at the chop shop, Cam was drinking a beer on his front lawn. I pulled up on the dirt driveway leading to his garage, which he had converted into a makeshift shop. His expressionless face, combined with the beard and large aviator sunglasses he wore, always made it difficult for me to read him. He was much older than the rest of us. Though he wasn't a big guy, he commanded a lot of respect among the guys.

Cam didn't wave, even when he saw that it was us. Through the rear-view mirror, I glanced at the empty dirt road behind us.

"We ran into some problems," I muttered, as soon as I got out of the car.

"Were you seen?" Cam's voice was monotone. He slowly paced around the car, occasionally kneeling.

I glanced at the tinted windows, "Not likely."

His head moved slightly, like a nod, but I couldn't be sure. "I'll have this done in an hour. There's some Heinekens in the fridge. Make yourself comfortable."

A couple of other guys I didn't know were talking and drinking beer, their bodies leaning against a teal colored Ford Explorer. Dickie walked up to the guys, shaking hands with one of them.

"Jaxson, help me move this car. Let's go, folks!" Cam clapped, and the guys immediately dispersed.

"Hey, Logan. This is for you." Cam handed me a DVD player that looked brand new.

He rarely paid us with money. Most of the time he gave us electronics he didn't want to keep for himself. Sometimes the gifts were more extravagant, like quads and dirt bikes. None of us kept track of the gifts or the favors when it came to working for Cam. We accepted whatever gifts he gave us, and if we needed any favors, we just asked him for help.

"Thanks," I muttered.

My job was over. I used to watch them disassemble the car until the parts were scattered all over the floor and all that was left was the frame. This time I just wanted to go home. I watched Dickie help the other guys for a while until he acknowledged me with a glare. Stacks of CDs covered an entire six-foot table.

"You really shouldn't keep these. It's evidence," I said to Cam.

Cam picked one up. "No one's going to bother looking at these. Except me. I haven't gone through them yet. Whatever I don't want you guys can take."

"You know, you really worry me sometimes," I said.

"Dude, relax. Stop acting like a bitch," Cam said.

I chugged the rest of the beer and crushed the can. "Thanks for the beer. I'm done."

"I need you here tomorrow. We're going to–"

"Not your bitch anymore, Cam. Gonna have to find someone else."

"You had a close call, and you're going to quit? Are you growing a conscience?" Cam laughed.

Dickie stopped what he was doing and watched us. We stood silently amid the sound of power tools and metal being stripped away from the stolen vehicle.

"I'm not getting–" I started.

"Go home, Logan," Dickie said. He went back to work, rolling himself beneath the teal car. His orange imitation Chuck Taylors stuck out, making me think of the witch when she was crushed by the house in *The Wizard of Oz*.

A part of me wanted to yank him by the feet and get him out of there, but Dickie was right. I understood that the first time you hesitate, it's over. But I also knew that even if I left, Dickie was going to stay.

His twin, Levi, was the first to call me when the police recovered Dickie's body. There had been no sign of foul play, so they concluded it was an accident. Dickie drank too much. He wasn't a strong swimmer, Levi said. Everyone said those things to make themselves feel better. No one will ever know the truth. All I could think about were his gangly legs sticking out beneath the SUV the last time I saw him. He just wasn't smart enough to know when it's time to quit. But I also blame myself. I should have stayed that day. I was the one who always looked after him. Maybe I would have made a difference.

## EXTRAS

*Daniel*

"So, your mom told me that you're an actor!" Holly held the bowl of mashed potatoes toward Daniel.

Daniel shrugged his shoulders while taking the bowl from her. He studied her face, which he thought was very pretty, in a wholesome, "girl next door" sort of way.

"You have to excuse my mother. She likes to exaggerate a little," he said. "I'm an extra. It's just a hobby for me. I always wanted to know how they produced TV shows and movies."

Mrs. Levinson dabbed the small speck of cranberry sauce on her upper lip with her napkin. "I think you would be an excellent actor if you chose to be. You've certainly always had the charisma. Plus, you steal every scene you're in with those good looks of yours."

"Yeah, he gets his handsome looks from me," Mr. Levinson interrupted.

Daniel's father was an average-sized man of five feet ten. In actuality, Daniel looked nothing like his father. Mr. Levinson hated to exercise and accepted his extra pounds and inches to his waist as something that simply came with age and maturity. Daniel, on the other hand, was innately athletic and played many types of sports as a child. Although he no longer played sports, Daniel regularly worked out at the gym four times a week, which afforded him a fast metabolism and a toned physique. Even he was aware that his naturally boyish good looks and trim figure gave him an edge at auditions.

"Where do you work?" Holly asked.

Daniel had just stuffed a forkful of mashed potatoes into his mouth. He smiled guiltily and tried to chew quickly.

"He takes people's blood," his father answered for him.

"I'm a phlebotomist," Daniel corrected and looked at his father. "And it's consensual, thank you very much."

Daniel wished his mother hadn't set him up with her friend's daughter for Thanksgiving dinner. He really wasn't interested in getting involved with anyone. He liked his life the way it was, but he also didn't want to hurt Holly's feelings or cause a conflict between his mother and her friend.

"Daniel, you should tell her about your latest movie project," Mrs. Levinson suggested.

Holly turned her face toward Daniel with excited expectation. His appetite vanished completely, and he worried that he might have to vomit.

"It's actually a television series. Nothing important. I'm just in the scene for a minute or so."

Most of Daniel's roles were playing one of the people in a crowd. Sometimes he got lucky on smaller production sets, and he was assigned a part where he was clearly visible in the scene. One time, they even gave him a line to say in the scene. This last role was different for him, however, and he didn't want to share it with anyone.

"Well, what's the show about?" Holly asked lightly touching his arm.

"It's a new series that takes place in Ancient Rome. The show tells the life of Commodus. He was the son of Marcus Aurelius."

"Oh, I love historical fiction!" Holly clasped her hands together.

"Me too," chimed in Mrs. Levinson. "His father and I watch history documentaries all the time."

"What role did you play in this show?" Holly asked.

"I just play one of the townspeople. A couple of the Emperor's advisors interrogate a senator."

Daniel had, in fact, played one of the townspeople, but the scene took place in a brothel. One of the Emperor's advisers storms into a brothel, hoping to catch one of the senators in a compromising position. Among the several rowdy men and women in the room, Daniel was situated in the corner of the room fornicating with one of the women. Though his back was facing the camera, someone more intimate with him could recognize him and his naked tush among the revelry of all the patrons.

"Was it exciting?" Holly asked.

"It's not bad." Daniel struggled to find the words. He hadn't thought much about doing the scene at the time. He and the woman, who was an aspiring actress working at a nightclub, enjoyed a few jokes as they waited to do their scene. She was so comfortable in her own skin that any awkwardness Daniel felt was significantly lessened.

He didn't plan on telling anyone of this recent performance, but when his mother had asked him to watch their house the same weekend the scene was filmed, he told her that he won a part as an extra.

"When does this series air?" Mrs. Levinson persisted.

"Yes! I want to see it. It sounds great! I've never known anyone who was on a real TV show," Holly added.

"Oh, the show won't be released for a while. I think they're still filming and then it takes months of editing. You probably won't even see me. Sometimes they even cut out my scene. Sometimes they even drop the whole project." Daniel desperately tried to think of something else to say to change the subject.

"What's the name of the series, sweetheart? That way she can look for the show when it comes out," Mrs. Levinson suggested. She got up to get a paper and pen so that Holly could write the name of the show.

Daniel worried that the perspiration on his upper lip was visible. He was never comfortable with lying.

"I don't know the name. I don't think they had an official name yet. They keep changing it." Daniel reached for the red wine that Holly had brought and filled his glass. He didn't even like wine, but he needed something to do. "Enough about me. You had mentioned earlier that you also worked in the medical field." He took a deep breath.

Holly's eyes lit up and her smile seemed to broaden, seemingly touched that someone was asking her a question about her own life. Holly easily chatted away about her career as a medical researcher. The wine started to take its effect on Daniel. His relief was so great that he half listened to Holly and his mother carry the conversation for the rest of the dinner.

*Ashley*

It was silent but deadly.

Ashley jabbed her elbow into boy sitting next to her in the back seat of a Chevy Tahoe.

"Ouch! That's actor misconduct!" the boy cried. His name was Josh.

"Do you know that every time you fart, you release fecal particles into the air?" Ashley hissed. The moment she laid eyes on this boy she knew he was going to be excruciatingly annoying.

"Don't panic! It's organic," joked Trey, who was sitting on the other side of her.

Trey and Josh guffawed, high-fiving each other in front of Ashley's face.

"I'm going to kill you," Ashley said intensely.

The actor playing the role of their father opened the door to the driver's seat. His body jerked backwards from the potency of the stench.

"She said she's gonna kill me," Josh dramatically whined.

"Yeah, I'll help her," the "father" responded, sliding into the driver's seat. "She's been stuck in the back seat of an SUV between two smelly boys. Disgusting."

"I think I smell like a peach," Trey chirped.

Ashley rolled her eyes. She had been so excited when she heard she got the part in the car commercial. She had never acted in a commercial. Yet, this experience was a far cry from what she had expected. They eliminated her line, so now she was just supposed to play a smiling, happy teenager, sitting between her wonderfully sweet brothers. Ashley wondered if the casting director was asleep when she selected the three of them. She didn't think she looked anything like Josh or Trey. She certainly didn't smell like them.

The director walked over to the car, carefully leaning a sleeved arm against the car. His eyes widened subtly because the smell was still lingering.

"You're getting paid and are very lucky to even be doing

this work. Knock it off," the director warned the boys sternly. "We start shooting in two minutes."

"I'm counting every second," Ashley said under her breath as soon as the director walked away.

The actress who was playing their mother gracefully hopped into the passenger seat. Her strong perfume made Ashley want to puke.

"Wow! You three back there were busy marking this car," the actress quipped.

"It was him." Ashley nodded toward Josh. "I'm just an innocent bystander who's trapped.

"You must be an only child," the "father" replied, looking at her from the rearview mirror.

"Yes, and I thank my mother every day she didn't give me a sibling," Ashley answered curtly.

"I'm one of six kids–" the "mother" started to say.

"Quiet on the set!" The director's assistant shouted. "Get ready! Action!"

For roughly thirty seconds, Ashley, Josh, Trey, and the mother sat quietly and still, superficial smiles plastered on their faces, while the "father" drove down a stretch of road nestled between thick forests. It took Ashley a lot of restraint not to look toward the window, where a camera car drove in perfect sync with them. She was just as interested in the production of filming as she was in acting.

They performed the stunt several more times, which Ashley thought was absolutely ridiculous, since they would probably only be on screen for a couple seconds. When the director finally decided he had enough material, the "father" parked the car toward the side of the road. There was a six-foot ditch less than a foot away from the Chevy Tahoe. Josh scooted out of the car carefully so as to avoid slipping into the ditch. When he saw Ashley get out of the car on his side, he tried to slam the door on her. She quickly stopped it with her foot and gave it a push. The car door hit Josh in the chest, causing him to stumble into the ravine.

Josh screamed and everyone rushed over to see if he was all right.

"I think I broke my leg," Josh complained.

"You're standing on it. You're fine. You just made an ass of yourself, that's all. Get out of there and we'll have the nurse take a look," the director said.

Josh wiped his nose with his arm, clearly embarrassed. When he climbed out of the ditch, he looked back at Ashley, who cocked an eye brow as if to say, "What? It's your fault."

After that Josh behaved himself and released no more foul air.

*Lindsey*

Wrapped in cheap and itchy muslin, Lindsey fantasized taking a long, hot shower. She had gotten up at 3:00 a.m. that morning to drive two hours to a filming location, where she waited another four hours to see if she would be one of the lucky people chosen to be an extra for the martyr scene, where the lead actress would be beheaded by a very convincing and elaborate guillotine.

Lindsey had always wanted to be an actress. When she was four years old, she asked her mother to take her to an audition for a cereal commercial. Her mother resisted at first, but Lindsey was so persistent that her mother finally caved in and even entertained the thought that perhaps her daughter was going to be a successful actress, as a result of being so strong-willed. Being extroverted and possessing a talent for imitating people, Lindsey initially won a lot of lead roles in plays and even a few commercials. However, the roles dried up when she reached high school. Though she continued to hold her own in her high school drama department, she never reached the same level of success again.

"What could possibly be taking them so long?" A woman standing behind Lindsey complained.

"Miss Eleanor must be having a meltdown because they didn't stock her dressing room with the right bottled water," a male voice added.

The man and woman were referring to the lead actress, who was playing the role of Eleanor. Lindsey had actually admired this actress, who was quickly becoming an A-list movie star. A dribble of sweat was working its way down Lindsey's temple and neck. She was wearing three layers of cheap muslin fabric. She was supposed to look like a commoner from a small, eighteenth-century French town. Her mouth felt dry, and she blissfully wondered what it must feel like to be successful, to surpass that point where enough people liked you that you could make money with your talent.

Lindsey carefully wiped the sweat from her face. She wanted to keep her face looking fresh for the scene. Since she was standing close to the guillotine, she was hoping that this scene might get her some attention. She had once read that Gene Tierney's career began when she was spotted simply carrying a bucket of water across the stage. Anything could happen.

Another hour passed and still no Eleanor. Lindsey felt that her ribs would never feel the same after wearing the most tight and uncomfortable corset she had ever worn. Her admiration for the actress was rapidly waning.

Finally, she heard shouting from some of the crew members, and the crowd of extras hushed. Lindsey's heart quickened as she saw the cameramen positioning the cameras in her direction. She swiftly smoothed the frizzy hairs around her forehead and patted her face with her sleeve to lessen the sweaty shine on her forehead and cheeks.

Another twenty minutes passed. Lindsey almost didn't notice the actress walk past her. The actress was so much smaller and thinner than Lindsey had expected. She wore a white shift and a wig that made it look as though her hair had been roughly shorn from her scalp. Makeup was expertly applied to the actress's face and body to make it look like she had been brutally beaten. Her appearance was sobering to Lindsey. She admired actors who were willing to sacrifice their beauty for a performance. Lindsey hated to feel vulnerable, and she wondered if she could really take on a role that unmasked the layers of what she felt made her socially acceptable.

The actress was already in character. Her walk, her stance, even her empty, pitiful facial expression was unlike anything Lindsey had ever seen in the tabloid magazines.

"Quiet on the set!" the director shouted.

The actress turned her back toward the crowd for a moment and then she turned around at the director.

"Action!" he shouted.

A combination of admiration and envy consumed Lindsey. She forgot about the camera, the uncomfortable corset, and the smell of the sweaty extras standing around her. She couldn't take her eyes off the actress. She forgot where she was. When the camera slowly panned over to Lindsey, her face was turned toward the direction of the actress, looking completely away from the camera. What she had hoped would be her big scene, was actually a shot of her hands, wringing tightly in front of her bodice.

## THE THREE PHILLIES

Ellie refrained from poking Dr. Bloom's rotund belly with her index finger. For the last few years he repeatedly told her that she needed to lose weight. Now, weighing five pounds less, he told her she was "too thin" and that her cholesterol was "too high." With his pudgy frame and doughy complexion, Dr. Bloom reminded Ellie of the Michelin mascot, though Dr. Bloom was not nearly as friendly looking.

"So, what are you three Phillies doing today?" Dr. Bloom asked, referring to Ellie and her two friends at the Philadelphia nursing home. He finished writing the prescription and handed the slip to Ellie.

"The same thing we do every day," she answered, reluctantly taking the slip. "Isn't there something I could take that's natural? I'm taking so many."

"Like I've always said, every drug has 'other effects.' But I wouldn't worry. I'd give this to my own mother," Dr. Bloom replied.

Ellie's jaw clenched, her lips forming a thin pink line on her face, but before she could respond, Dr. Bloom had turned his back on her, rushing off to see the next patient.

* * *

Their names were Ellie, Bess, and Marty. Ellie had just turned eighty-five in June; Bess was ninety; Marty, the oldest, was ninety-two. Sometimes it seemed as if they were related, their short (none of them even reached five feet), delicate bodies shuffling down the hallway with walkers as though they all had some immediate purpose. But they came from different parts of the country, and they had lived very different kinds of lives. Marty had been a professional violinist who performed with the San Francisco Symphony; Bess had been a nurse for fifty years; and Ellie had worked as an elementary school teacher at a public school. When they moved to the Linda Jay Assisted Living and Nursing Home seven years ago, they seemed to gravitate toward each other like magnets, practically becoming inseparable.

Linda Jay was better than most old-age homes. There were far worse facilities out there, where the stench alone was enough to make someone dizzy. When Linda Jay first opened, it was only for assisted living care. All the patients were required to walk and climb stairs without the assistance of a walker. But since Linda Jay had switched management, the facility expanded to include patients who needed more care. Another building was added, with hallways lined with dormitory-size rooms. With the influx of new people, sometimes two residents were assigned to a room, as long as they could tolerate each other.

The rooms and hallways were always kept clean. Claire Larson, the bubbly and energetic event coordinator, planned different activities every week, like lectures and bingo. But in the end, Linda Jay was still a nursing home and there was no pretending otherwise.

The bond Ellie, Marty, and Bess had developed and even

their gossip somehow shielded them from the pervasive bleakness that seemed to overwhelm everyone else. The three of them were always together, gathering in the sitting area every day for an hour or so before lunch and dinner, talking about their latest ailment or their families. They kept track of who was new at Linda Jay and who was aging faster. Marty even had the knack for guessing who was "headed out the door." She was openly proud of the fact that she was the second oldest patient at Linda Jay, and she always tapped on something made of wood when she talked about making it to a hundred so that her name would be mentioned on the *Good Morning America* Smucker's list. Though the three Phillies were confronting their impending mortality, they still somehow managed to look forward to tomorrow.

"How was your doctor's visit, Ellie? Here, take this pillow for your back. They put too many pillows on these couches," Marty said, pulling the cushions from behind her back and tossing them on the seat next to her.

"I'm fine, Marty. I don't need a pillow," Ellie said, kicking out her thin legs, which didn't reach the floor. "The doctor says my cholesterol is high, so he's making changes to my diet. But my blood count was good, so I guess I can't complain too much."

"No more eggs for you then. You love your omelets," Bess said, smoothing the wrinkles on her slacks. She always dressed nicely, even if it was just to come downstairs for lunch in the cafe.

"She can eat egg beaters," Marty suggested.

Ellie snorted, crinkling her face. "I'm not eating that crap. One of these days they're going to come out with a study showing how bad that stuff is. I'll find something else. I can still eat bagels and toast. Maybe my cholesterol will go back down, and I can have eggs again."

Marty and Bess nodded thoughtfully.

Howard, one of the newer patients at Linda Jay, walked into the sitting area. He was a warm, talkative fellow who made sure he greeted everyone he saw. He suffered from the moderate stages of Alzheimer's. Sometimes he made the rounds two or three times before one of the nurses took care of him.

"Well, hello, ladies. How are you doing this afternoon?" His voice was raspy, as if he were recovering from laryngitis. His back was hunched over, and he had to hold on to the back of the couch to keep his balance.

"We're doing just fine, Howard. We haven't seen you in a couple of days. I hope you're doing okay," Marty said.

"I caught a cold last month, and I couldn't leave my room. It just about wiped me out, but the doctor gave me a clean bill of health. Thank you for asking, Linda."

"Marty."

"Uh-huh. Well, it's been good to see all of you. I'm going to see how Bill is doing," Howard said.

"Bill? But Bill passed—" Bess started.

Ellie put her hand on Bess's arm and discreetly shook her head. Howard's attention drifted away, but the women couldn't tell where he was looking. Howard headed toward the hallway with a distressed expression spreading on his face. Before he reached the exit door, one of the nurses approached him, gently touching his arm and speaking to him in a soft, reassuring tone.

"That poor man," Marty said, still watching the nurse calm Howard. "Remember when he first got here? His posture was so straight, and he looked pretty good. Now he's all hunched over, and his condition has gotten a lot worse, don't you think? He's got one foot out the door. It's a shame. He's only seventy-nine. Can you imagine? I'm several years older than him, and granted I have my ailments, but at least I can say I'm doing all right." Marty tapped the "wood" coffee table with her knuckles.

"As long as I have my mind, I think I can handle the other problems. I simply wouldn't know what I would do if I didn't have my memories. That's all I have left," Bess said.

"At least he's lived a full life. Not everyone is lucky enough to reach old age," Ellie retorted.

"When is Stephanie coming to visit you?" Marty asked.

"She should be coming this Saturday. It's every other weekend. Nothing's changed," Ellie said.

"That's nice. She's such a sweet, mature girl. You don't find too many kids like her these days," Bess said.

Ellie fidgeted with a loose thread on her blouse. Her stomach was feeling unsettled again.

"I think she's been going through a rough time. She should be socializing with her friends. She needs her mother. This isn't a place for a teenager. I love her company. She's the highlight of my week, but I want her to be happy," Ellie said thoughtfully.

Had she looked up she would have seen the slight envy flickering in Marty's eyes. Marty loved children, and not having any of her own grandchildren, she lived vicariously through Ellie's relationship with Stephanie. Every time Stephanie came to visit, Marty shuffled down the hallway, her face beaming as though her own grandchild was coming to see her.

"You know how many of these people would kill to have their grandchildren visit them. I don't think they get even a phone call from them. You're lucky," Bess said.

"I never pushed myself onto my family. I was there for them when they needed me, but I always gave them their space. I've watched some of these people put guilt trips on their families: 'You don't visit enough.' 'Why aren't the children calling?'" Ellie altered her tone, imitating some of the patients.

"Well, excuse me," Bess retorted. "I think I do a pretty good job giving my family space, but sometimes they're so wrapped up in their own lives that I don't think they would ever call me if I didn't give them a nudge once in a while."

"And what's wrong with Stephanie putting a smile on our faces? I wish there were more people like her. Besides we're good company, aren't we?" Marty said.

"All right. All right! I'm sorry I said anything," Ellie said wearily.

Stephanie was Ellie's only granddaughter. She was thirteen, but she could have passed for eighteen. In one summer she grew five inches and matured into a young woman. She was a pretty girl, with a face reminiscent of a young Judy Garland. While she came to see Ellie, she also enjoyed interacting with the other patients at the nursing home, especially Marty and Bess. She was not like the other visitors, who felt obliged to visit their relatives. Most of them were uncomfortable, folding their hands on their laps and tightening their lips into thin lines until the visit was over. Stephanie was like part of the crew. She engaged all the patients, even the more challenging ones who suffered from dementia. She could listen to the same story multiple times and fool them into thinking she had just heard it for the first time. But while she put smiles on these patients' faces, she was also getting something in return. For those few hours she was the center of attention. They gushed over her youthful face, grabbed her smooth hands, and continually praised her maturity. These compliments and the way that so many of them expressed their excitement when they saw her gave her emotional nourishment.

When Stephanie arrived promptly at noon on Saturday, her father came with her. He was a six-foot-tall version of Humpty

Dumpty, a barrel on two pegs. His face always looked like he had just smelled something sour.

"When you're done with your visit, can you meet me at the guest parking lot? I don't want to go through all that construction again," her father complained.

Stephanie nodded quietly, signing in at the front desk. Marty rounded the corner first. She let go of her walker for a moment, spreading her bony arms out like she was going to envelop Stephanie.

"Oh, look at you! It's so good to see you. Ellie will be here soon. She was finishing getting dressed. How are you, Mr. Hirsch?" Marty said.

"I'm fine, Marty. Thank you. Stephanie, give me hug. I'll see you later," he said.

"Don't you want to say hi to Baba," Stephanie asked, giving her father a quick hug.

"I need to finish that report today. I'll say hello next time. Have fun." He waved to Stephanie and Marty, making swift strides toward the door.

Just as Mr. Hirsch disappeared, Ellie appeared. Her usually reserved demeanor melted every time she saw Stephanie. Her shoulders lifted, her mouth smiling broadly, like she was going to giggle. Gripping the walker, she wrapped one arm around Stephanie, who nearly had to double over to accommodate the difference in height.

"I hope you're hungry, sweetie," Ellie said as the three of them walked toward the dining room. With its white and stainless-steel decor, the room looked like a hospital cafeteria.

"I'm starving. I skipped breakfast," Stephanie said.

Ellie paused to give Stephanie a disapproving glance.

"I'm trying to lose weight," Stephanie confessed.

"You look fine, dear. Like a tall drink of water," Marty said.

Bess joined them in the dining room, carrying her grocery

bag stuffed with lavender yarn and knitting supplies. While they were still reading the menus, the waitress rushed toward their table, pulling out her notepad.

"I'm going to have an iced tea and the Cobb salad," Ellie said.

"Sorry, Ellie, but you're not allowed to have eggs. You could try the grilled chicken salad or the tuna salad sandwich. I hear that's pretty good," the waitress responded.

Letting out a long sigh, Ellie skimmed through the menu again. She selected the grilled cheese sandwich and handed the menu to the waitress. As soon as the others ordered, the waitress ran to the next table.

"It was worth a try," Ellie said, the left side of her mouth lifting.

"They're like nuns here. I feel like I'm ten years old again when they tell me I can't have something," Bess complained.

"I can't believe you can't eat eggs!" Stephanie shook her head. "At least they're natural. I don't understand how they can be bad for us. Dad just made Pop-Tarts illegal in our house. The sweetest thing we have in our kitchen right now is Raisin Bran. I hate that cereal. It turns to mush as soon as you pour the milk," Stephanie said. She pulled out her cell phone to respond to a text message. As her fingers moved rapidly, Marty shook her head in awe.

Stephanie's dexterity with her smart phone was inexplicable to these women. But yet the three of them seemed enraptured with her personality as they listened to her talk about her life at school and home.

"What's wrong, Bess?" Stephanie said, catching her staring at two elderly women sitting several tables away from them.

Bess carefully set down her knife and fork on the plate and wiped her mouth with the corner of the napkin.

"When I first moved here, people got dressed up when

they came downstairs. Now you see it all. That woman over there looks like she's in her pajamas. When I was young, you dressed nicely to go out. No one dresses up anymore. Even at the theatre, people wear dungarees and shorts. Sometimes I just don't even bother coming downstairs because it's depressing to see people not care how they look."

"Every weekend, when I was about your age, Stephanie, the whole family got dressed up to go out for Sunday brunch. It was a big thing in my family," Marty said.

"I don't like dressing up." Stephanie smiled and confessed. "I just want to be comfortable. If I could, I would live in my pajamas." They all laughed.

Ellie sighed. "When I was young, I used to like getting dressed up, but I'm old now. I could care less if I ever get dressed up again. I just want to be comfortable now."

Though Bess didn't say anything, she pursed her lips as though to suggest she obviously didn't feel the same way.

After lunch the women crowded into Ellie's small room. The room was sparsely decorated with a twin bed, chair, and small dresser supporting a TV. She used every wall and surface space to display photographs of her family, particularly Stephanie and her mother, Meredith. When she thought no one was looking, Stephanie would look at the photographs of her mother as a young girl. Ellie noticed, and it warmed her heart.

Before her recent surgery, Marty would play a few songs on her violin or, since Stephanie was taking violin lessons, teach her some scales. Afterward, the four of them would play cards. Lately, however, Stephanie's favorite activity was watching old movies with Ellie. Mr. Hirsch had bought Ellie a DVD player for Christmas so that the two of them could watch movies. Every visit, Stephanie brought a different movie to watch. Now she was obsessed with any movie starring Esther

Williams. She liked watching the synchronized swimming. As they watched, patients and some of the older nurses wandering down the hallway would drift into Ellie's room.

"My wife looked just like her when she was young. I always said that Esther Williams was prettier than Elizabeth Taylor. Look at those legs! Whew!" Lewis was another fellow resident at the facility. For several minutes his eyes were glued to the TV, his body swaying slightly to the music. Occasionally, Stephanie looked at him, happy she could witness this joy. Finally, when the movie was over, Lewis meandered back to his own room.

Ellie relaxed on her bed while she watched the movies. She stole glances at Stephanie who sat in the only chair, leaning her elbows on her knees, her gaze fixated on the screen.

"Did you ever like to swim, Baba?" Stephanie asked as the credits rolled.

"Honey, I was terrified of the water ever since I was a small child. You couldn't get me to go near it. There was no reason for me to be afraid. I feel bad that I never learned because I couldn't teach your mother. She didn't learn until she met your father."

When it was time to leave, Stephanie lingered around the black and white photographs of Ellie's parents and older brother. She carefully picked up a framed photograph of Ellie's brother wearing a black suit and tie.

"Do you think about him a lot?" Stephanie said.

Ellie pushed herself off the bed, clutching the walker. Sometimes she forgot that she had these pictures. Running her finger lightly over the glass, her mind travelled back in time.

"Sometimes it doesn't feel like they're really dead. They're always alive in my mind," Ellie answered.

"I think it's harder for the people left behind," Stephanie said.

"It certainly feels that way."

Ellie hoped that Stephanie's interest in the photograph was an indication that she wanted to talk about her mother, but the expression of concern disappeared from Stephanie's face.

"I'd like to bring *West Side Story* next time," Stephanie said.

"That's fine. Your mother loved Natalie Wood."

Stephanie swung her backpack over her shoulder and gave Ellie a hug before she left. Ellie couldn't tell for sure, but she thought she saw the corners of Stephanie's mouth turn upward, just a little.

\* \* \*

Several weeks passed, and Stephanie continued to visit Ellie every other Saturday. Ellie tried her best to be patient with her granddaughter, but as she watched her collection of DVDs grow, she began to fear that Stephanie would never be ready to talk to her about what was on her mind.

As they were watching a movie, Ellie saw Stephanie drawing on her arms with a permanent marker. She immediately chided Stephanie, who tossed the pen in her bag. Five minutes later she caught Stephanie again doodling on her jeans with a ball point pen.

"What? It washes off," Stephanie argued.

"I don't care if it washes off, you shouldn't be drawing on your body or your clothes. Why don't you sketch in your notebook?" Ellie said.

"Never mind." Stephanie slid off the chair and lay down on the floor, staring up at the ceiling.

For a moment, Ellie felt helpless, not knowing how to respond. Her chest seemed tight, and her whole body felt too warm.

"Benjamin would have turned eight this year," Stephanie said several minutes later.

"That's right. It'll be eight years August 4th," Ellie sighed.

The details of that day were still so clear in Ellie's mind compared to all the years that had passed since Meredith's death. She was living in her apartment at the time. Every morning she watched her favorite talk show while she drank her coffee. She took care of all her errands and chores in the morning in case her daughter needed her to pick up Stephanie from school.

When Mr. Hirsch called her that morning, she knew something was wrong. His words were slurred, and he was sobbing. He didn't mention Meredith immediately. He repeatedly asked Ellie to meet him at the hospital where Stephanie was admitted for a concussion and broken arm.

"Where's Meredith?" Ellie had said for the fifth time. Her hand shook so badly that she spilled the coffee all over the table.

"She was crushed from the impact. There was nothing they could do to save her," he said.

"But where is she?" Ellie demanded.

"She's dead, Ellie." His voice broke.

"Damn it, Robert. Where's Meredith? Where's my baby?" she screeched, pounding the table with her fist.

Meredith was seven months pregnant and thirty-eight years old when she died, but she was still Ellie's baby. The police officer who was on duty had called it an act of God. A tire from an SUV exploded, causing the vehicle to careen into Meredith's compact sedan. Ellie squeezed her eyes shut, shaking her head vigorously. She refused to hear the rest of the details about the accident. Ellie's grief took its toll on her, and less than a year after her daughter's death, she submitted an application to move into Linda Jay Assisted Living.

The past seven years were siphoned from Ellie's memory and put in a place she couldn't access. Every day spent in the nursing home was added to a collection of other colorless, uneventful days. Every year the pile of forgettable days got bigger, until the years became indistinguishable to Ellie. She wasn't miserable in the nursing home, but it was as if her internal life were dull. She could never recover from her daughter's death. Though she looked forward to Stephanie's visits, she was growing more comfortable with her mortality.

Stephanie picked up the pen again, drawing amoeba patterns on her jeans.

"Please stop drawing on your clothes. What's on your mind, honey?" Ellie coaxed.

"Nothing," Stephanie muttered.

"You can always talk to me." Ellie thought to press further, but, as Stephanie tightened her grip on the pen, Ellie stopped herself. She didn't want to distress Stephanie, but at the same time she knew she had to help her grandchild.

Ellie forced herself to relax so that she wouldn't make Stephanie nervous. The silence between them weighed heavily on Ellie, and she found it difficult to breathe. There was nothing in the room or anything she could do to distract her attention, so she sat perfectly still, enduring the discomfort.

"You mean I can talk to you about Mom," Stephanie said after a while. "Dad doesn't like to talk about her."

"He doesn't like to talk about the dead. Most people are uncomfortable talking about death," Ellie said.

"And what about you? Doesn't it bother you to talk about it?" Stephanie asked.

There was a long pause. At first Ellie didn't know how to answer the question. The honest answer was too complex and difficult for her to share with a teenager. As she tried to find the right words, she lost track of time gazing out the window.

When she finally started to speak, she felt like hours had passed.

"A parent never gets over the loss of their child. To be honest, I never discuss your mother with anyone. Even after all these years, it's still hard. But I'll talk about it with you because she's your mother, and I think you need to be able to express your feelings."

"I think Dad feels angry that Mom died and I lived. He was really excited about Ben," Stephanie said.

"How can you say that, Stephanie? He loves you just as much. I don't think he would have been able to keep going if something had happened to you, too."

"But maybe it was my fault that she died."

"How so?"

"Because I didn't want a younger brother. What if–"

"No, Stephanie! That had nothing to do with what happened. There are many children who aren't thrilled about having a sibling. It's an adjustment, and your parents understood that."

"But Dad is always miserable, and I can never make him happy. I could do ninety-nine things right, and he'll look at the one thing I did wrong," Stephanie complained.

Ellie laughed, and Stephanie's eyes widened.

"I hate to tell you this, but your father has always been moody. The accident changed him, but he's still the same person. We all have our *foibles*, as my mother would call them, and that doesn't change even when we love someone."

Ellie looked closely at her granddaughter. She wondered what Stephanie was thinking just then. When she didn't say anything, Ellie pretended to turn her attention to the TV.

"I wonder a lot what life would be like if she were still alive," Stephanie said quietly.

When Ellie turned back from the TV, Stephanie was

looking away from her. She was sitting up now, her legs tucked toward her chest and her arms wrapped tightly around her shins. Maybe she was looking at the photographs on the dresser, but it was hard for Ellie to be sure. She desperately wanted to put her arms around the girl, but something about Stephanie's demeanor prevented her. Stephanie wasn't reaching out to her, like Ellie had hoped. For a moment, a feeling of anger coursed through Ellie's body. Ellie was old and tired and she was more than aware that she couldn't help Stephanie the way Meredith could if she were still alive. Ellie took a several breaths to calm her heart.

"She gave you the best parts of herself," Ellie finally said when she recovered.

"I like to think so." Stephanie smiled and gave her grandmother a hug.

At first Ellie was surprised when she felt Stephanie's arms wrap tightly around her. Ellie had never dealt with her own grief, and she worried that it dampened her emotional response to Stephanie. By getting Stephanie to talk about her mother, Ellie was also helping herself. She hoped that maybe they would be able to talk more over time. It was a start.

Later, when Mr. Hirsch came to pick up Stephanie, he waited in the lobby. He smiled warmly at Ellie, but he still kept his distance. Ellie wondered if her face looked as sad as his. She waved goodbye to the two of them, the words of love and gratitude trapped behind tightened lips and sorrowful eyes.

# HOLY WATER

I n the second to last row of the cube farm a note on fluorescent yellow paper was taped onto the partition separating the last cubicle: DO NOT TAP ON GLASS. DO NOT FEED BEAR. The note was written in bold block letters.

With the exception of the note, the desk looked like all the others in the call center. There was a phone with a headset and a computer.

This particular desk belonged to the newest member of the Castor Call Center, Billy Gaston, extension 4412. The company was small, with only fifty employees. Castor took calls for small businesses in the southwest region.

Next to the water cooler hung a poster-size bulletin announcing the Employee of the Month. Samantha Hardwick was the current winner. There was a candid photo of the young woman wearing a headset and giving the thumbs up. Billy tried hard to imagine his face on the bulletin.

One of the employees slapped Billy on the arm and said, "Welcome to the farm. No one lasts here more than three months."

He walked over to the glass case near the entrance of the building, which displayed all the products the call center handled, including Sammy's Vegetarian Diet Shake, Mineral Makeup, Adult Toys by Suzy Q, and Manny's Holy Mineral Water. Billy's tall frame leaned over the display. He stared at the middle shelf with the pyramid of pale blue water bottles next to the assortment of colorful adult toys.

"You like that? I just finished redoing the display. I've always liked setting up the merchandise. There's an art to it, you know." The young man put his hands on his hips, shifting his weight to his left leg. His name was Brian. He was in charge of coaching Billy, after Billy had completed a week-long training session.

"But holy water? From Sedona? I thought you weren't supposed to drink water that is holy." Billy looked skeptical.

"Yeah, I know. What can I say? It probably comes from someone's bathtub, but the company is still our client. You're here to sell the product." He patted Billy's shoulder. "My desk is just next to yours, so I'll be checking in on you to make sure you're not having any problems."

Every morning Billy was the first person to arrive at the call center at 7:50 with his green hoodie (the call center was always kept at sixty-eight degrees) and a thermos filled with coffee. Halfway into folding a sheet of paper into an origami frog, the first call of the day came in. He fumbled with the headset, making sure that the microphone was positioned in front of his mouth.

"Hello. My name is Billy. How can I help you?" He had a baritone voice that was monotone. He enunciated each word carefully.

"Uh. . . I wanted to order the Dainty Butterfly." The woman said it more like a question than a request.

"Can I get your name?" He clicked on the website, so that he could place the order.

"Pixie Granger," the woman said in a barely audible whisper.

"*Pixie*–I mean Ms. Granger. That comes in ocean blue, luscious purple, purrfect pink, or—"

"Blue's fine," she responded quickly.

"Okay, Ms. Granger." He filled in the information on the website as quickly as his thick fingers would allow. "Your purchase today comes to $22.99, which includes shipping."

He collected her credit card information. Repeating each piece of information back to her.

"Is there anything–" She had hung up the phone before he could finish. Billy leaned back in his seat, letting out a long, loud sigh. He was required to say the customer's name three times throughout the call. He could barely remember the customer's name, much less remember to say it three times.

Someone tapped on the partition. Billy jumped in his seat, pushing the headset off one ear. Brian's head was visible from the nose up.

"Hey! Not bad. Don't forget to upsell with the Lucy Lube." He winked at Billy.

"Okay. Thanks, Brian." Billy leaned back in his seat for a moment. The phone rang again.

"Hello. My name is Billy. How are you doing today?"

"Uh, hi." A man's voice answered. "I just saw an ad for Sammy's Vegetarian Diet Shake, but I have a couple of questions."

"Sure. What can I help you with?"

"What kind of protein do they use for this shake?" The man spoke slowly as though he wanted to make sure Billy caught every single syllable.

"It's rice protein, sir," Billy answered. He was relieved it was an easy question.

"Is it gluten free?

"Yes," Billy answered again.

"Soy free and dairy free?"

"Yes to both."

"Is it yeast free too? My doc doesn't want me eating yeast. It clogs my tum tum," the man said.

With his index finger, Billy underscored the ingredients. No one had ever asked about yeast. "I don't see it listed in the ingredients."

"Is it made with *all* organic ingredients?"

"Yes, sir," Billy said a little wearily.

"I'm not really a vanilla or strawberry person. Is the chocolate any good?"

"Chocolate is actually our best seller."

"Can you use this shake as a meal replacement or is it just for snacks?"

Billy rubbed the bridge of his nose. "I think you can use it for either a meal or snack, whichever works best with your diet."

"I'm working with a nutritionist, and she wants me to get twelve grams of protein and twenty grams of carbs every four hours, you know, to keep my blood sugar level," the man responded.

"I'm not a dietician, but it says there's eighteen grams of protein and thirty grams of carbohydrates in one scoop."

"Hmm . . . One scoop. So I guess I could do ¾ of a scoop. That would be pretty close, I think. Hmmm . . . Well . . ."

"You could give it a try, and if you don't like it–" Billy started. Suddenly, he heard a woman shouting in the background, but he couldn't completely make out what she was saying.

"Maisie, I'm on the phone!" The man yelled. Billy pulled the headphones away from his ears. "What, Maisie? Oh!"

"Sir?" Billy asked.

"Sorry, son. My wife just told me she found it on Amazon for less money. Thanks!"

Before Billy could interject a word, the man hung up. He began to understand why no one had lasted longer than three months in the call center.

"One of those, huh? I hate when they just use you for information." It was Brian's voice from the other side of the partition.

Billy felt drained, but his line started to ring again.

"Another customer, Billy. Chop-chop!" Brian cried enthusiastically.

"Hello. This is Billy. How can I help you?"

"Oh! Hi, Billy." The woman's voice was shrill, with a noticeable New Jersey accent. Billy guessed that she was middle age. "I thought you were going to be a girl for some reason."

"So did my mother."

There was a moment of silence that felt awkward to Billy. He was beginning to feel that he was not cut out for this job. He drummed his fingers against the desk, wondering what he would do if he lost this job. He heard the woman clear her throat.

"Well," she began, "I saw this advertisement last night when I was watching my show. Have you tried Manny's Holy Mineral Water? The man in the ad said that it helps with clarity and brain function."

"No, ma'am. I haven't tried it yet."

"Well, maybe I'll wait and order another time. Seems awfully expensive for just water."

"Oh! But it's not just any water. It's . . . it's actually *blessed*. Manny's Holy Water has received hundreds of positive reviews from customers who have purchased this product. Many have stated that it has changed their life."

"Hmph! I really don't believe that water from some hippie town can be holy. There has to be something in the water to make it that special."

Billy's eyes crossed, and his thoughts scattered. Laying his hands flat on the table, Billy stretched his fingers wide. There was a fine white line that traveled up his middle finger on his left hand, the result of an accident when feeding the pigs at his uncle's farm.

He stared hard at Manny's website searching for any description that might help him glorify the product, but he couldn't find anything particularly exciting to explain why this water was really special.

Feeling determined to find the tipping point to make the sale, Billy took a deep breath and said, "This water is different because Manny uses a completely different process than other water companies. It's just as purified and safe as Dasani and Aquafina, but it's what happens after the bottling process that makes this water *special*. The water is stored in a spiritual room in one of Sedona's internationally known churches. The water is blessed and surrounded by prayer for thirty days before being shipped to customers. The results have been astounding."

"What kind of results?" The woman asked.

"Expanded consciousness," he said weakly.

"What do you mean?"

"Well, s-some people have reported that they have had visions," Billy said. He knew this was a lie, but the mounting pressure to make the sale was steadily increasing so that his head started to ache. Maybe if he had a few good calls, Brian would be impressed. His fingers were tapping the desk frenetically. If he were going to lie, he knew he had to be consistent and give just enough information to be persuasive.

"What kind of visions?" The woman asked.

Billy could detect a slight lilt in her voice, and he felt encouraged.

"They saw their loved ones who had passed on." He slowed down to reduce the stuttering.

"My husband Stephen died seven years ago from a heart attack. It's been very lonely."

"Well, this one man saw his wife sitting one night in her usual chair like nothing happened. She just kept talking about a trip to the Caribbean that they were supposed to go on before she died. She kept telling him he better pack his things so he could go on that trip."

"And did he go on that trip?"

"He sure did, ma'am."

"Please, call me Phyllis."

"Well, Phyllis, he ended up going on that trip to the Caribbean and had the time of his life. He even met another woman, so he's not lonely anymore."

"I've been lonely. But now why didn't they share this in their advertisement? I didn't hear anything about visions. You make this water sound better than the man on TV did."

Billy rolled his eyes, hating himself a little. He picked up a pen and started doodling on his notepad. "Not everyone has visions. However, almost all our customers experience clarity and improved brain function."

"I'll be sixty-eight this fall. I'm always trying to keep my mind active. They say that's the best way to prevent Alzheimer's. My memory's not what it used to be. Sometimes I'll get up to go grab something, and by the time I get there, I forget what I was going to grab. Maybe I should try this water."

"You won't be disappointed, Phyllis. Would you like a package of six, twelve, or twenty-four? With the largest package, you save five dollars. Plus, the shipping is free."

"Then I'll start with twenty-four."

"I highly recommend that. Also, let me take this opportunity to share some of our other products. Manny also sells Blessed Trail Mix."

"What does it taste like? Is it any good?"

Billy wiped the beads of sweat accumulating on his forehead. He was so close to the finish line. "Like God's nuts."

Brian snorted loudly from the other side of the partition.

"I don't know . . ."

"I'll tell you what, Phyllis," Billy began. "If you purchase Manny's Holy Mineral Water and Blessed Trail Mix, I'll throw in the Banana Rama Manna Bread for free. It's tasty, organic, and high in fiber. You'll never feel toxic again after you try this bread. This is a one-time deal." Billy was practically hyperventilating.

This was another lie, of course. The bread was thrown in for free with any purchase of Holy Water. Billy heard Phyllis sigh.

"I suppose I'll give it a try. I'll purchase the two items."

"Fantastic, Phyllis. Let me get your address and credit card information, and I will send that to you right away."

"This better be good water," she said just before she hung up.

Billy leaned back in his chair, letting his head drop and his eyes close. His ears itched, and he rubbed them fiercely. When he opened his eyes, he saw Brian leaning over him. He held an imaginary cigarette between two fingers and nodded toward the back door.

"But I don't smoke," Billy said, getting up from his seat and following Brian outside.

Brian kept his gaze on Billy as he lit his cigarette, inhaling and exhaling dramatically. He ran his hand through his dirty-blond hair. He was a solid head shorter than Billy.

"God's nuts, Billy? Really?"

"You told me to do whatever was necessary to sell the product."

"Yes, yes. That's true, but I didn't mean for you to jump the shark. Visions? No one has had as much as a moment of brilliance from this water. We can't make claims like that or we'll get in trouble. Look, Billy. I know you're trying real hard to do a good job, but I think I need to work with you a bit more–"

"No. I quit. I'm not cut out for this." Billy took a step back and held out his hands. "I sit in a chair for ten hours, in a freezing room, helping people buy crap that's not even going to make them happy or better. I lasted almost two weeks. That's good enough for me."

"Where are you gonna go?"

Billy shrugged his shoulders, "I haven't figured that out."

Billy gathered his belongings. It was lunchtime, and many of the employees were leaving for lunch. Billy didn't bother to say good-bye to anyone. He wanted to disappear from this place. Sitting in his Dodge Neon, Billy kept his head slightly bowed so that his skull wouldn't brush the ceiling. He couldn't decide where he wanted to go. He kept driving west, away from the city and toward the green expanse of farmland. He turned the car down one of the dirt roads between two cornfields. Tiny rocks from the dirt kicked up, making a pinging sound against the bottom of the car.

At the end of the road, he put the car in park and got out. Inhaling deeply, he smelled that particular scent that only the dirt out here had. Billy couldn't describe this smell, but he could describe in great detail the satisfying memories that flooded back into his mind every time he was out in the field.

# AROUND THE FUR

S unny's bottom began to itch. His skin hadn't yet hardened to the rough fabric of his yellow bear suit. He tried jumping and shimmying a little, his guitar swinging over his white tummy. Nothing was working. He gave up after a while and focused on the audience, a mass of people dressed in a plethora of plush animal suits in an assortment of colors. The anonymity was intoxicating to Sunny. He wanted to run across the stage, jump off the monitors, and dance like Angus Young from AC/DC. He did his best to emulate his rock heroes, but the heavy weight of the suit exhausted him.

When it was all over, Bobby Blue, the lead singer of Around the Fur said good night to the crowd and announced the date for the band's next show. Instead of clapping, the audience cheered and hollered, as most of their hands were covered in paws. A swarm of giggling furry fans surrounded Bobby. A gray and white cat lunged through the circle and wrapped its arms around Bobby's neck. The bass player and drummer, Ruby Red and Violet Purple, immediately hobbled off the stage, leaving Sunny by himself. He had no idea what to do with himself now that they were done performing. He squatted down on the edge of the stage, pushing in the belly of his costume so he could see what he was doing. The cumbersome suit was too big for him, throwing off his coordination. His right foot caught on the cord, and he tumbled onto his back, his limbs swinging in the air. For a moment, the house music was absorbed with hilarious laughter and jeering.

Sunny pushed himself up and slowly slid off the stage. He wanted to tear off his costume and scratch his skin until it bled. He wondered who had worn this suit before him. The interior had a funky odor.

He shuffled through the cluster of furries. A group of them had formed a circle in the center of the floor. Tigger was breakdancing in the middle, swinging his tail like a boa. Some of them had started to clap or tap their feet to the music. Tigger bounced high in the air, contorting his body in strange postures, but always landing perfectly on his feet. He rolled onto his back, swinging his legs in the air until the momentum spun his body like a top.

Across the circle from Sunny, a life-sized version of Raggedy Ann swayed to the tempo. The bulbous head piece covered in a giant mop of red yarn dwarfed the girl's body. Her slender legs were covered in red and white striped tights. Sunny froze. He didn't move, not even when Tigger strayed too close to the edge, accidentally kicking him in the groin. Sunny doubled over, clutching himself and moaning.

"Sorry," Tigger said quickly, returning to his routine.

Sunny slowly stood up. Raggedy Ann was gone. He stepped out of the circle to find her, but she was nowhere to be seen. Was she a figment of his imagination? He finally caught sight of her red and white legs climbing the stairs to the upper level.

"Excuse me. Sorry," Sunny said repeatedly, squeezing his way up the steps. He wasn't used to being this large.

The upper floor was divided into multiple rooms. He

stared at the closed doors, his right foot rubbing his left knee. Sweat dribbled down his torso and legs. Ruby and Violet came out of one of the rooms, their arms linked. There was a stain on the front of Violet's suit. They passed him, without as much as a gesture of acknowledgment.

He opened the door nearest him. The room was dark and saturated with loudness and sweet-smelling smoke. The whites of the costumes were illuminated under the black light, the crowd appearing like Lilliputians gyrating to the Butthole Surfers. With his arms extended slightly in front of him, Sunny pushed his way through, a perfect oval of brightness in search of red-and-white striped stems. Something wet splashed his side. Someone's backside rubbed against him. He twisted his body this way and that, trying to find what he was looking for. When he felt desperate to escape, he couldn't find the door. He pressed himself against the wall, edging his way around the room, until he felt the doorknob poke his belly.

Sunny skipped the second door and trailed behind two furries headed toward the last room. Their bodies parted at the threshold, like a curtain revealing the show. Sunny immediately recognized Bobby's cobalt bear-suited body locked in a lustful embrace with Raggedy Ann. Sunny's shoulders sagged defeatedly inside his costume.

A pair of purple arms grabbed Sunny from behind. He couldn't turn his head far enough to see who was fondling him. A low male voice whispered to him.

"Hey, honey bear. I liked your playing." He pulled Sunny onto his lap. "Yellow is my favorite color."

Sunny propelled himself off the lap and turned around to see a purple furry, who was wearing an elaborate hippopotamus suit. Four plastic, bright-white teeth jutted out of the partially open mouth. There was a lipstick stain on one of the teeth.

Sunny felt like he couldn't breathe, and he instinctively

tugged at his costume. By now his clothes were soaked with his sweat, and his muscles ached.

Something caught the Hippo's attention, and he ambled to the other side of the room. Sunny took one last glance at Raggedy Ann straddling Bobby. He pounded down the metal staircase, sinking back into the entanglement of furries vibrating to the music.

The stage was dark now. All the lights were directed toward the dance floor. Sunny hoisted himself up to the stage and grabbed his black and white Fender Stratocaster. He played the first song that came to mind: The Fratellis' "Chelsea Dagger." The distortion was cranked high, inspiring Sunny to strum harder and faster. The house music lowered. All the furries turned around to watch the crazed, yellow bear headbanging, screaming the lyrics into the microphone.

When he had finished the song, he held the guitar over his head triumphantly. Some of the furries from the crowd shouted for him to play more. A piece of someone's costume flew onto the stage, landing near Sunny's foot.

"I'm done," Sunny screeched, smashing the guitar onto the ground. The amplifier shrieked with feedback as the guitar splintered into pieces. The cheering was deafening. Still gripping the broken neck of his guitar, Sunny walked off the stage. The audience parted, making a path for him. He didn't stop when a fluffy unicorn slapped him on his ass, or when Tigger said he was the bomb, or even when Ruby Red planted a kiss on his cheek. Sunny left the building.

He continued walking down the street, ignoring the stares from the pedestrians and honks from drivers. At the corner of Fifth and Jackson Street, Sunny turned around. Fire billowed from two trash cans. A group of homeless people sat nearby, seemingly oblivious to Sunny. He walked over to them, and pulled off his head piece. He cradled the head, contemplating the bulbous green eyes and broad, toothless grin.

"Why can't I be like everybody else?" Sunny thought. He had wanted to embrace a different identity, but sadly even anonymity couldn't help him escape from how he felt about himself.

The homeless man standing closest to the fire approached Sunny, "Do you have a cigarette?"

Sunny shook his head. He moved toward the trash can, the sweat on his face drying from the heat, and dropped the bear head into the fire. One homeless woman opened her eyes after waking up from the sharp, crackling noise. The flames soared, veiling the bear's face. After a while, all Sunny could see were those green googly eyes, winking at him through the fire.

He left the group and continued walking, still not sure where he was going. A petite figure layered in fabric was walking toward him. A round shape hung from her hand. They both paused. Their flushed faces lifted in surprise.

"Hey." They both said at the same time and smiled.

Her hand released Raggedy Ann's head. The soiled, grinning face of Raggedy Ann rolled across the pavement into a pile of discarded cardboard boxes.

# FIFTY-FIVE & OLDER

Every morning at 5:30, Adam heard the same woman's voice outside his bedroom window loudly coaxing her dog, Caesar, a small long-haired Pekinese, to hurry up and go to the bathroom.

"Come on Caesar! You can do it." Her high-pitched, piercing voice got even louder when the dog finished.

"Oh, Caesar! You're such a good boy! Who's my baby?" Now she was cooing.

Adam swore that her voice could even shatter the walls of Jericho. This interruption generally lasted for about fifteen minutes. Adam sometimes managed to fall back to sleep, only to wake an hour later.

"Jerk! . . . You don't pay the rent . . . wasting your money on that . . ." The shouting came from the woman who lived next door, arguing with her boyfriend. The only time she didn't yell in the morning was when she spent the previous night keeping Adam awake with her loud, euphoric screams.

Adam thought he had rented a "luxury" condo in a trendy neighborhood. The condo had all the appeal of a modern apartment, but the walls were exceptionally thin. When he stood in his tiny kitchen, just next to the refrigerator, he could even hear his neighbor's sneeze.

Adam rolled onto his side and squinted to read the numbers on the alarm clock. After spending ten minutes debating whether he should try to sleep another twenty minutes or get up, he threw the comforter off his body and slowly pushed himself out of bed.

For the past three years, Adam worked in the IT department for a human resource firm, so he mostly worked from home with the exception of when the problem required him to be at the office. While he logged onto his computer at 8:00 a.m., he made breakfast and watched the news.

After nearly five hours of answering tickets, Adam removed his headphones and did a few stretches to relieve the stiffness in his back and neck. Even though he was an introvert and preferred staying home, he felt like he was going stir-crazy. He put on some clean clothes and decided to walk over to the coffee shop that was within walking distance from his condo.

Just as he cut across the grassy area by his front door, he felt the bottom of his shoe step onto something squishy.

"Caesar! That damn dog." Adam cursed, scraping the dog poop off from his shoe. Weren't people supposed to scoop up their pet's waste?

By the time Adam got to the coffee shop, a posh-looking café that played house music that was a little too loud, he was sweaty, angry, and paranoid that someone was going to smell his neighbor's dog on him. While he stood in line to place his order, he observed the other patrons sitting at tables, their eyes either glued to their smart phones or their laptops. Even the people sitting with their friends seemed more interested in what was going on in their virtual world than engaging the old-fashioned way.

Most of the women were wearing gym clothes, or, as his sister called them, athleisure wear. A couple of them wore cropped, loose-fitting tanks that said Spiritual Gangster. Adam thought that sounded like an oxymoron. He thought yoga people were more inclined to be pacifists.

Three teenaged girls who were in line with Adam were so preoccupied with trying to take a group picture that one of them stepped on Adam's foot, coincidentally the same foot that had stepped in dog crap.

"Oh! I'm so sorry!" The girl exclaimed laughing.

"It's fine," Adam sighed, watching them immediately go back to attempting their group photo.

The young woman behind the counter didn't look up when she asked for his order.

"I'd like a medium latte and the pumpkin spice bread," Adam answered.

"Uh . . . okay. Medium latte and . . ." The woman looked up and sighed. "What was the other thing you wanted?"

"Pumpkin spice bread," Adam repeated more slowly.

As he waited for his order, he checked out the magazines on the display rack. One of them was a publication for real estate and property rentals. Although he had no plans of moving, he still enjoyed checking out other properties. His parents complained that he was too old to be renting and that he should settle down already and own his own home. The thought of buying made Adam feel claustrophobic. Despite the fact that much of his life was predictable, he still wasn't sure what he wanted out of life, and therefore, he didn't want to commit himself to a lifestyle that didn't fit who he was.

While flipping through the magazine, a photo of a luxurious and sleek-looking patio home suddenly caught his attention. He scanned the full-page ad, which showcased a patio home community that included a state-of-the-art gym, two resort-style pools, barbeque pits, a coffee shop and café, as well as an assortment of scheduled classes and activities. It also included three bedrooms, two and a half baths, and garage parking. The rent was a little on the high side for him, but he knew that if he made a few adjustments and tightened the proverbial belt, he could manage it.

"Adam! I've got a large latte." A different girl placed his order on the counter.

Adam quickly took a snapshot of the page from the magazine with his phone, not realizing that they got his order wrong. When he saw that they gave him a large instead of a medium, he laughed. At least this time the error worked in his favor.

Adam nearly forgot about the patio home until he was getting ready for bed and the couple next door started fighting. He picked up his phone to examine the snapshot of the magazine page. This time something caught his attention that he hadn't noticed before. He expanded the image, holding the phone closer to his face. The community was called Golden Heights, Resort Style Living for residents fifty-five and older.

He looked up the website for the community. The homepage displayed a montage of images showing off the amenities and beautifully furnished homes. Adam rarely ever used the oven, unless it was to heat up pizza, but even he was impressed by the sleek kitchens with brand new appliances. The bedrooms were spacious, and best of all, he wouldn't have to share a wall with his neighbor. Everything about this community was better than where he was living now.

He put his cell phone on the counter and looked at himself in the bathroom mirror. His dates frequently commented that he acted much older than his years. He was never sure exactly what they meant, but he thought it might have something to do with his obsession with Brahms and his extensive stamp collection. In two months, he would turn thirty-seven, which was kind of getting close to being forty.

Plus, he liked older people. He thought he might even have more in common with them than with his own generation. Older people liked to keep to themselves. He probably wouldn't ever see or meet his neighbors. Finally, Adam would get some peace and quiet.

Adam leaned toward the mirror and examined his hair. Over the past year, he bemoaned the rapid acceleration of gray hairs accumulating near his temples, but now he thought he could use a few more gray hairs. Turning to the side, Adam evaluated his physique, which was average for his 5'11" frame. With the right clothing and a little bit of hair dye, he could manage to age himself at least another decade or so. It was a risk, but one worth taking, he thought.

The woman next door started screaming and interrupted Adam's train of thought. Apparently, his neighbors had made up. One time Adam considered approaching her about her loudness, but when he saw that her boyfriend was a burly six-foot, three-inch specimen, he thought better of it. Instead, he increased the volume of his sound machine and smothered his head with a pillow.

During his lunchbreak the next day, Adam stared at the phone number he wrote down on a notepad. He took a couple of deep breaths before he dialed the number. He needed to make sure he had his story straight.

A man with a noticeable Bostonian accent answered the phone. "Golden Heights leasing office. My name is Greg. How can I help you?"

"Uh . . . hello. Yes, I'm calling on behalf of my father. He has to vacate his current residence on short notice, and I thought your community would be ideal for him."

"Great!" Greg responded. "Let's set up a time to meet so that—"

"Well, I'll be taking care of the rent and all the paperwork. It's really too much for him now. He's easily traumatized by information overload. If there's a way that I could handle it for him that would be preferable." Rivulets of sweat stained the front of Adam's shirt. The ruse hadn't felt real until now. Adam was unaccustomed to lying, and he was afraid he wouldn't be able to keep track of his lies.

"Typically we like to set up an appointment so that you, or in this case your father, can check out one of our model homes and meet our staff members. It's a really great community that helps give residents a chance to stay active. We're adding a bunch of activities this fall, like water yoga and more cooking classes."

Adam vigorously rubbed the spot between his eyebrows. He was starting to change his mind about pursuing this ruse. He didn't like to lie, and he knew that he was in over his head.

"It does sound wonderful," Adam said. "With my father's situation it's very hard for us to make an appointment right now. Thank you for taking the time to speak with me."

"Actually," Greg said, "we're a little short-staffed right now, and I leave on vacation next week. We can take care of this over email and phone. One of my associates can meet with your father later."

Within a minute after ending the call, Greg sent Adam a lengthy email with several attachments. At first, Adam felt overwhelmed by the situation he had just gotten himself into, but now he felt a sense of commitment to see this through.

By the end of the week and several emails later, Adam was cleared to move "his father" into a three-bedroom patio home in the quiet community of Golden Heights.

\* \* \*

A few days before the move, Adam heard a knock on his door. His older sister, Hannah, stood on his doorstep, holding a bag of groceries against her hip. Her usual cynical facial expression shifted into shock when she saw Adam.

"Oh my God! What happened to you? You look like you've aged twenty years!" Hannah exclaimed, covering her gaping mouth with her hand.

"Thank you! I've been working on it," Adam answered cheerfully. He grabbed the groceries and the two of them went in the kitchen, which was crowded with moving boxes and newspapers. Adam grabbed a couple of bottles of Diet Snapple for them.

"Mom was worried that you weren't eating properly so she wanted me to bring some organic food over to you." Hannah rolled her eyes. "If Mom saw you now, she'd want you committed. Is all that gray natural?"

Adam shook his head and smiled. "I found the most incredible place to rent, but it's for people over fifty-five. I'm trying to go for the distinguished, mature gentleman look. I just can't see myself wearing sweatpants, like Dad, so I ordered a few short-sleeve button-up shirts and a pair of New Balance sneakers."

For a moment, Hannah just sat silently, her lips slightly parted.

Adam continued, "And did I mention the house? It's awesome. Everything is brand new, and the room that I'll be using as my office is huge with a—"

"How did you get through all the paperwork? How are you going to blend in? You may look old, but you act like you were born yesterday," Hannah said.

"I used some of Grandpop's info. I remember his information from when I was taking care of him," Adam answered calmly. "I've also been watching classic movies and old sitcoms and listening to some of the musicians that were really popular in the fifties and sixties. You know, I think Frank Sinatra is starting to grow on me."

Hannah blinked a couple of times and shook her head. "A small part of me is rather impressed, but the majority of me feels horrified. You do realize that what you're doing is illegal, right?"

"I'm trying not to think about it." Adam sat down at the table and started peeling the label off the bottle of Snapple. "I honestly didn't think I would make it this far, but everything just kept opening up for me. I just feel like it's meant to be. Please don't tell Mom and Dad. I'll tell them myself eventually."

A loud reverberating thump rattled the kitchen wall followed by shouting. Adam's neighbors were fighting again. Hannah knocked on the wall, which seemed to put the fighting on pause. But just as Hannah winked at Adam, the neighbors recommenced their shouting.

"Okay. I'll keep your secret," she promised solemnly. "But please let me fix those highlights. The unevenness is killing me."

* * *

Adam could hardly believe his luck when he finally moved into his new residence. His nights were quiet and there were no dogs yapping him awake early in the morning. He reveled in the peace and quiet of his new home. Occasionally, he'd spot one of his neighbors from afar when he collected his mail.

Adam always smiled, but he was careful not to engage with anyone. He wasn't in any hurry to pretend that he was part of a different generation.

One morning, as Adam was getting ready to work, he heard a knock on the door. His body went rigid, and he didn't move until he heard another round of insistent knocking.

He opened the door just enough so that his body was blocking the view of the inside of his house.

"Good morning, Mr. Jorgenson!" The woman standing in front of him was dressed youthfully in capri jeans and a bright orange tank shirt. Her makeup and hair was obviously done up to make her look younger. She carried a large Pyrex pan of what looked like lasagna.

"Um . . . hello," Adam replied more as a question.

The woman held out the pan toward Adam, smiling brightly, "My name is Suzy. I just heard that we had a new neighbor, and I wanted to give you a warm welcome. I live two doors down. By the way, I hope you like lasagna. It's my mother's recipe, and it's always been a success, so I'm sure you'll like it."

"Th-thank you very much," Adam stammered. "It's very nice of you."

"I'm so sorry. It looks like I just woke you up," Suzy said, still smiling.

Instinctively, Adam ran his hand through his hair, feeling embarrassed that he looked disheveled.

Suzy laughed coquettishly and touched his forearm. "Don't feel bad! I'm an early bird. I just love the mornings! I'm on my way to a cooking class at the activity center. You should join us for one of our classes. Our teacher is a top-notch chef."

"It does sound wonderful, but unfortunately I have to work today," Adam replied.

"What do you do?" Suzy asked.

"IT–I mean I work with computers," Adam answered, feeling overly aware of how young and uncertain his voice sounded.

Suzy laughed again, "I know what IT means. My son is a software developer for a big tech firm in San Francisco."

"Oh. . ."

"I'll stop by in a few days to see how you liked my lasagna. Now remember, if you need anything, I'm just two doors down. By the way, you should think about joining us some time at the activity center. We're really a nice bunch of people." Suzy winked and walked back to her car. Even her step had a slight bounce, which Adam thought was unusual for a woman her age.

Adam made room in the fridge for the lasagna and, for a moment, he stared at the dish as though it were an intruder. His brief exchange with Suzy had been his first foray into this community. He wasn't used to pretending to be someone he was not, and he hoped that he hadn't aroused any suspicion. In his mind, he retraced everything he had said. What would he do when she came back?

His cell phone went off, vibrating idly on the kitchen table, and for once he was grateful for the distraction.

Two hours later, Adam heard another knock on the door. He broke out into a cold sweat as he walked toward the front door. He took a deep breath and tried set his posture as though he were imitating his father.

"I'm so sorry to bother you. Suzy told me you work with computers and for the life of me I can't get on the Internet and my computer is just so slow. But really I just need to get on the Internet so that I can fill out these medical forms for my doctor's appointment tomorrow. The receptionist told me that the doctor won't see me unless I get these forms to them by the end of today."

The woman spoke fast and Adam could tell that she was distressed. He was accustomed to working with people who were easily intimidated by technology.

He pulled his cell phone out of his pocket to check the time. "I have a few minutes. I can take a look and see if I can help, Mrs.—"

"My goodness! Where are my manners! You can call me Rita. I live next door to you. You don't know how much your help means to me."

Adam followed Rita toward a house that was a mirror copy of his, except her house was much cleaner and filled with furniture that looked expensive. Two Scottish terriers ran up to him barking and then sniffing his ankles as he followed Rita to a home office where her computer was set up. Adam immediately went through the steps of determining Rita's problem. While he was waiting for the router to reboot, he heard a door close.

"Jerry!" Rita called out. "Is that you? I need you to bring me a glass of water. We have a guest. Our amazing neighbor is helping me with the computer."

"What's wrong with the computer?" Jerry shouted back.

Moments later, a man that looked about the same age as Rita entered the room holding a glass of water. As soon as he spotted Adam, he straightened his posture just ever so slightly so that Adam noticed. The man's facial expression was stern and completely devoid of warmth.

"Hi, I'm Adam," Adam weakly raised his hand to wave. "I'm almost done here. It shouldn't be more than a couple of minutes."

Rita grabbed the water and put it on the desk for Adam. "Take your time! You're so sweet to help me. I'm so glad to know someone who understands technology. I just never know what to do when this happens with the computer."

"You call the Internet provider. That's what you do," Jerry retorted.

"Well, I went to our neighbor, Jerry, and I'm glad that I did. I think it's important to know who's living next door. By the way, Adam, be careful around Suzy. She's very, very sweet, but she's also very aggressive when it comes to men, if you know what I mean."

"Rita, he's our age. He's been around the block. I'm sure he knows how to handle himself around women."

Adam felt a pang of sadness and confusion. Even though he wanted to pass as an older man, a part of him also felt bad that he so convincingly looked the part.

"Where's Julia?" Rita asked suddenly.

"She's putting the groceries in the fridge, then she's heading back to her place. She's choosing Netflix over her parents." Jerry answered, adding some sarcasm toward the end.

Julia stormed into the office. She wore a black tank shirt, jeans, and black combat boots. Her long, wavy hair was partially pulled back with a clip, and her arms were crossed over chest. Adam noticed she had a tattoo on the inside of her forearm, but he couldn't make out the design.

"I just want to enjoy my own company. I'm tired of watching old movies where everything has to have a happy ending. That's not how life works," Julia said.

Rita looked apologetically toward Adam, shaking her head. "You'll have to excuse my daughter. She just turned thirty, so she's not in the best mood."

"Mom!" Julia yelled, but she was looking right at Adam, who had forgotten that he had not stopped looking at Julia since she had entered the room. He quickly averted his gaze, horrified at what Julia must be thinking about him right now.

"Everyone turns thirty at some point, if they're so lucky. You're still young." Rita turned once again toward Adam, addressing him this time. "Tell her that thirty is young. She never believes her parents."

Adam wished that Rita hadn't dragged him into the conversation. All he wanted to do was disappear.

"Someday you'll look back and realize how young thirty is," Adam answered awkwardly because he remembered thirty being a hard birthday for him as well.

Adam thought he detected some disdain in her eyes. Rita walked over to her daughter, affectionately putting her hands on Julia's face.

"What he means to say is that you should be grateful," Rita started. "Your life is just beginning. Now, don't forget your groceries this time. You don't want to have to drive all the way back here."

"Your computer is back online, ma'am—I mean—Rita. I can let myself out," Adam sputtered.

"Don't be silly, Adam. Julia, give me a couple minutes to walk our neighbor to the door. He's been so especially helpful this morning."

While Rita led Adam to the front door, she apologized again to Adam for witnessing a glimpse of their family chaos.

"Don't worry about it. Every family has some drama," Adam said.

"I have three daughters. Julia is my youngest. When one child isn't happy, I'm not happy. Sadly for me, my girls are never all happy at the same time."

Nearly every week, Adam's sister called to "check in on him," although he secretly believed Hannah was gradually becoming more interested in the retirement community.

"It's Dad's birthday this weekend, and he just wants a quiet family dinner at the house. So be there at 6:00 p.m. on Sunday," Hannah said shortly.

"I can't. Mom will flip out if she sees me like this."

"Well, you should've thought of that before you decided to pass as a geriatric," Hannah snapped.

"Please help me get out of this. I know it's Dad's birthday, but things are going so well here and I don't want to ruin it," Adam begged.

"No. Besides, I'm looking forward to watching you try to explain this to our parents."

"Is there any chance I can change your mind? Like a bribe?" Adam pressed, but his sister didn't respond right away. "Hannah?"

"Yeah. I'm thinking if there's anything I want. Hmmmm . . . nope. I'll see you Sunday."

"Thanks a lot," Adam retorted.

"Why don't I come over before dinner, and I can help you look a little less atrocious. I have some temporary dye and–"

Adam looked at his watch, "We'll have to talk about this later. I have a cooking class soon, and I need to leave."

"You're taking cooking classes?"

"Suzy–I mean my neighbor–kept pushing me to take the cooking class, and it seemed easier to just give in and try the class. It's actually pretty fun. We're learning how to make dumplings today."

"You're engaging with these people?" Hannah asked, sounding horrified. "You've never liked engaging with your neighbors. What's happened to you?"

Adam sighed. "When I spend time with these people, I forget after a while that they're decades older than me. They're just people, and they happen to be kind to me. They say hello when they see me. It's nice to feel a part of a group."

"I guess I understand how you feel, but I still think it's not going to work," Hannah said.

\* \* \*

Adam felt leery about letting Hannah see his new home, even if it was to help him look more presentable to their parents. He chose to wear a baseball cap that would at least hide most of the gray hair. There was nothing he could do about his beard, which at this point was thick and transformed his boyish face. Just before he knocked on his parents' front door, he forced himself to take a couple of deep breaths and try to remember how he stood and moved before taking on his new identity.

His father answered the door and there was that awkward moment when Adam thought for sure his father would make a remark about his new appearance.

"Happy birthday, Dad," Adam said uncertainly and held out a wrapped present for his father, which was a signed photograph of Mickey Mantle.

"Thanks, son." Adam's father took the gift, but he was still scrutinizing his son's face, particularly the full beard that Adam had never worn. "Go help your mom. She's finishing making dinner."

As was per the usual Sunday evening, classic jazz music, such as Ella Fitzgerald and Sarah Vaughn, played in the background. When Adam walked into the kitchen, he saw his sister and mother pulling out the plates and silverware. Simultaneously, Hannah and his mother froze when they noticed him.

"Oh!" Adam's mother said breathlessly when she finally recovered from her shock. "I know facial hair is popular now, but I don't think the beard suits you."

Hannah rolled her eyes and mouthed "good luck" to Adam.

"I'm trying a new look. Something low maintenance because I've been working a lot."

Hannah snorted, and their mother looked at the two of them suspiciously.

"Well, I just don't like it," his mother said haughtily. She handed the silverware to Hannah so she could take the brisket out of the oven. "George! Dinner is ready!"

George ambled into the kitchen and sat down at his usual chair, which was not at the head of the table. That particular spot was reserved for Adam's mother, Maggie, who frequently got up from the table to grab one thing or another. In general, Maggie was a spry, older woman who couldn't sit still.

The first ten minutes were fairly quiet, with Maggie asking Hannah about her job and her best friend, who recently found out she was pregnant.

"So, what's up with the new look? Are you trying out for the part of Moses?" George asked.

"No. I'm going *au naturel*." Adam grabbed a dinner roll from the basket and stuffed a large piece into his mouth so he wouldn't be able to speak.

"I think it's the stress from his work. He doesn't get enough rest," Maggie continued.

"There might be a supplement or some kind of vitamin to slow down the effect of graying. In fact, I think I read that B vitamins can help prevent or reverse gray hair. I should look into that," George pondered, cutting a generous slice of butter for his dinner roll.

At this point, Hannah rolled her eyes dramatically, clearly losing her patience. She reached over the table and pulled Adam's baseball cap off his head. "Just so you know, he's passing for a creepy old man so he can live in a senior center."

At that precise moment, Maggie was taking a generous sip

of her drink, and the liquid went down the wrong pipe and she violently coughed multiple times.

"A nursing home?" George said, horrified.

"It's a retirement community." Adam turned in his seat to glare at his sister. "You couldn't even make it an hour."

Maggie cleared her throat. "But there are so many other places to live. Why choose a retirement community?"

"I just really like the community. The house is the most beautiful place I've rented. The neighborhood is quiet, and I don't get woken up in the middle of the night by my neighbors. Don't worry. I *can* afford it. It's really not that big of a deal," Adam answered.

"Yes it is," George interjected. "If they find out your age, you'll be in some kind of trouble."

"That's why I'm very careful."

"No, you're not," Hannah argued. "You're taking cooking and yoga classes with that woman."

Maggie gasped, and she placed her hand over her chest as if the shock caused her heart to race. "Is there a woman in your life? An older woman?"

"Well, there goes our chance of passing on our family legacy," George said solemnly.

Hannah slammed her hand onto the table. "Hello? My name is Hannah, also known as your other child."

Adam raised his voice. "There's no woman. I just take a couple of classes with my neighbors. They're old enough to be my mother. I promise there's nothing going on. Besides, I think they're very nice people. After a while, I forget about the age difference."

For a moment, no one spoke. Hannah and George went back to eating their dinners, but Adam's mother stared glumly at her plate, and then she started to cry.

"Mom, there's no need to cry. Please don't cry," Adam pleaded, glancing at his sister for help.

"Some birthday this turned out to be," George huffed.

"In Adam's defense, the house is really beautiful. All new appliances and granite countertops. Plus, he's finally learning how to cook. That will come in handy one day, I'm sure." Hannah picked up her wine glass, holding it up to the light as though she had wanted to examine its color. "Of course, I look forward to seeing the house sometime. Adam says I can't visit because he'd have to tell people I'm his daughter."

A few more sobs escaped their mother's lips. "I just want you to be happy, Adam. I feel like I failed you as a mother."

"I am happy. You didn't fail me," Adam said. "When I get settled, I'll have you all over for dinner, and you'll see that it's like every other neighborhood."

"Except devoid of children and young people," Adam's father added. "Now, can we talk about something else so I don't have to hear your mother cry all evening?"

"Oh, George! Don't be so melodramatic." Adam's mother brushed away a stray tear just beneath her eye and got up to get the birthday cake ready. Just like that, Adam's mother recovered from her shock. "Hannah, why don't you take the ice cream out of the freezer and grab some candles."

After George opened his gifts, Adam made an excuse that he needed to leave early to finish up "some work" he had due on Monday morning. As Adam put on his coat, his father approached him.

"Look, son. We don't mean to be too hard on you. Your mother and I really just want what's best for you. I'm just concerned," Adam's father said.

"I'm not going to live there forever. I just really like the house, and I'm happy living there. It's going to be fine." Adam zipped his sweat jacket and gave his father a quick hug.

"Happy birthday, Dad. Try not to worry so much. People are too concerned with their own problems to care about how old their neighbor is."

"Just be careful, Adam. The truth always tells on itself," his father warned.

\* \* \*

Despite the fact that Adam had considered himself to be an introvert and homebody, his social life continued to expand within his new community. For the first time in his life, Adam got to actually know his neighbors. As soon as people learned that he had computer skills, many of the women called him for assistance or advice. When Mrs. Ryden's knee gave out, Adam got her mail and threw out her garbage. He even took her to the orthopedist twice.

Sometimes the husbands eyed Adam suspiciously, but Adam made sure not to give them any reason to worry. And yet, his popularity with the women in the community continued to increase. He even modified his work schedule so that he could join his neighbors for the water aerobics class to work off all the cakes and treats the women gave him when he fixed their computers. He was happier than he had ever been. It might not have been totally real, but the feeling was real.

Adam savored his Sunday mornings. After he made a large cup of coffee, he went to his office, which he had set up with dual computer monitors and expensive speakers. On one monitor he played *South Park*, and on the other he logged into a computer game. He had only been playing for fifteen minutes when he heard the doorbell ring followed by several quick knocks. He initially ignored the knocking, but it continued and he quickly padded down the hallway to the front door.

"Be right there!" He yelled as he quickly tied his robe to hide his Batman T-shirt and plaid boxer shorts.

As soon as he had opened the door, he knew something was wrong. Rita's face was contorted with shock and fear.

"Oh, thank goodness you're home! Jerry and I were running errands this morning, and he collapsed. The ambulance is taking him to the hospital, and I came back here to get some of his things. But now my car has a check engine light on. I don't know what that means. I hate to ask this of you, but could you give me a ride to the hospital? I'll have Julia pick me up later." Rita's hands were trembling as she fumbled with the straps of a large tote bag.

"O-of course!" Adam stammered. He looked down and realized he still wasn't dressed. "Just give me two minutes."

"May I please sit on your couch? My heart is racing, and I just need to sit down for a moment." Rita took a step forward, already assuming that Adam would invite her into his home.

Adam stepped back awkwardly as Rita let herself in and sat down on his sofa. Up until this point none of the neighbors had been inside his home. He glanced at the game controllers sitting next to the television and the Captain America movie poster that he had purchased at Comic-Con and wondered if the small details of his generation would attract Rita's attention and be his downfall. However, she was sifting through her tote, apparently oblivious to his obsession with gaming and Marvel comics.

As soon as he found a pair of clean jeans and a plain T-shirt, he ran back out into the living room to find Rita with her arms crossed over her chest and staring at a pile of freshly laundered clothes sitting on his kitchen table.

"You know my husband did the same thing when I first met him. I had to train him, poor man," Rita said.

"I apologize. I'm behind on my cleaning this week." Adam

saw that a pair of boxer shorts were absurdly lying on the very top of this pile, and he grabbed a towel from the pile to cover the clothes. "Anyway, I'm ready to go. Rita? Are you okay?"

Rita seemed frozen in place as her thoughts were elsewhere. Just as Adam considered gently tapping her shoulder, she snapped out of her momentary trance.

"Yes, yes. We need to get going."

Adam expected that Rita would have been quiet on their ride to the hospital, but instead she talked the entire time they were in the car. She enumerated the things they had been doing that morning and their fateful trip to the hardware store, where Jerry collapsed in the plumbing aisle.

"Jerry has arthritis in both knees and these low toilets are just too hard for him. That's why we were at the hardware store to buy a taller toilet. I know low toilets are supposed to be better for your stomach, but I just think his knees would be happier with a taller toilet. I thought he was pretending to have a heart attack when I told him the price of the model I wanted, but then he fell to the ground, and I felt terrible." Rita rummaged through her purse until she found her cell phone. "Excuse me, Adam. I need to take this."

"No problem," Adam answered, rubbing one of his sweaty palms against his jeans. He quickly glanced at Rita as she talked on the phone. Now he noticed that her makeup was smudged, probably from crying. He had no idea what to say or do to make her feel better, and he felt incredible anxiety toward hospitals. The only time Adam went to the hospital was to say goodbye to his grandfather after he suffered a massive stroke. He was terrified of hospitals, but he wasn't going to let Rita know that fact about him.

When Adam pulled up to the hospital entrance to let Rita out of the car, she put her hand on his shoulder and gave it a squeeze. "Thank you so much, dear. You have no idea how much I appreciate you driving me here. I really shouldn't be behind the wheel right now." She quickly gathered her things and rushed inside the building.

As Adam pulled the car out of the parking lot, he saw an orange bottle of pills roll across the floor on the passenger side. He let out a frustrated sigh and drove back to the hospital. An administrator at the front desk told him to wait in the lobby, and she would send a message to Rita. By now, Adam was in a cold sweat, and he wished he had a jacket while he sat in the refrigerated sitting area. He pulled out his cell phone to play a game so he could try to distract his mind from Rita's husband and the goosebumps forming on his arms.

"What are you doing here?" Julia stood in front of him with her arms folded over her chest. Adam could now see the distinct resemblance between Julia and her mother. They both had an authoritative presence, which slightly intimidated Adam.

"Your mother needed a ride to the hospital, and this fell out of her bag." Adam held out the bottle of medication.

Julia plucked the bottle from his hand and read the label. "Oh. That was nice of you."

She sat down in the chair next to him and covered her face with her hands. Adam felt sympathy for her and he wanted to say something to her, but he was pretty certain that she wouldn't want comfort from him.

Adam stood up and put his hands in his pockets, "Well, I guess I should be going. Please tell your mother that my thoughts and prayers are with your family."

Julia looked up at him. "Do you mind staying until my Mom comes back? I think I'm having a panic attack." She was breathing heavily.

"Oh. Sure. Of course." Adam sat down with his hands folded in his lap and nervously looked in her direction.

The two of them sat there silently for a few minutes. Adam tried not to watch her too closely, but he could hear her taking long, deep breaths.

"I'm sorry I'm not really helpful. I never know what to say," Adam admitted to her.

Julia sniffed and rubbed her eyes. "It's okay. Sometimes there's nothing anyone can say."

Adam saw Rita on the other side of the lobby, and he stood up to wave to catch her attention. Rita walked over to the two of them, and Julia handed her the bottle of pills that she had dropped in Adam's car. Rita embraced her daughter and repeatedly whispered, "Daddy's going to be okay."

Rita let go of Julia. "Adam, I don't know what I would do without you. The doctors are doing some tests on his defibrillator, so I'd like to get some coffee because I think it's going to be a long day today."

"Is Dad awake?" Julia asked.

"Yes, but he's really out of it right now. He hit his head when he fell, and so he also has a concussion. But I think he's going to be fine. He's hardheaded, that's for sure."

The three of them went to the cafeteria where Rita bought them all something to eat and drink. They chose a table that was by the window and away from other people.

Rita looked at Adam as she plopped into her seat. "Aging is a bitch, isn't it?"

"It definitely sucks," he responded.

Rita pulled out a photograph from her checkbook wallet and laid it on the table. A young Rita was smiling brightly for the camera. Her face was much fuller back then and her hair was styled in a puffy flip like the fashionable hairstyles of the 1960s. Jerry looked much different with his full head of very dark hair and slim figure. However, Adam noted the same serious facial expression Jerry always seemed to have.

Rita tapped the photograph with her index finger. "I first met Jerry when I was fourteen and he was seventeen. He was a lifeguard at the public pool in my neighborhood where I grew up. Of course, we didn't date until I was sixteen, but this is from when he took me to my junior prom. Look at how handsome he was. We've been together for so long, I sometimes feel like we're one person. I just wouldn't know what to do without him . . . but he's going to be fine. The cardiac specialist is taking good care of him."

"Dad's too young to die," Julia said.

"Honey, he's going to be sixty-six this year. Your grandfather was sixty-five when he died. Once you reach your sixties, you grow to appreciate each day. You start getting more aches and pains, and you wonder if it's normal or if you should start worrying. . ."

Adam's mind drifted away from the conversation going on between Rita and her daughter. Jerry was the same age as his parents. He never really thought about his parents dying someday. He took it for granted that they would always be around. He simply couldn't imagine a world without them. Now he felt overwhelmed at the thought that someday he would have to face that reality, but hopefully not for many years.

"You're never ready to lose your parents," Adam heard Rita tell Julia.

When it was time for Rita and Julia to check on Jerry, Rita gave Adam a hug. She was roughly the same height as his mother and the way in which she tenderly embraced Adam felt comforting and familiar to him.

"I'm so sorry for taking up so much of your Sunday. Thank you for being there for us, Adam. Please take care of yourself," Rita said.

"It's really no problem. Let me know if you need anything,"

Adam told her. He was surprised at how much he really meant it.

* * *

As it turned out, Jerry did recover, and after a couple of days he was back home resting, which Adam had learned when he was at their house fixing another computer problem for Rita.

"You again," Jerry said as he shuffled past the doorway of the office.

"I'm glad you're feeling better," Adam responded, smiling. He was used to Jerry, and he even found his curmudgeonly manner endearing in an odd sort of way.

When Adam finished with the computer, he let himself out so he could return to his own work without further distraction.

"Adam!" Rita called from the front door. "Don't forget the cooking class! You don't want to miss this one. We're making kouigns."

"Sure thing. I'll be there," Adam promised, even though he had no idea what a kouign was.

As usual in the class, Adam was stationed at the middle of the table surrounded by the women in the complex. While Adam was adept with anything related to technology, he was an absolute mess in the kitchen. In cooking class, he always managed to get flour on his face, forearms, and even his beard was speckled with powder. The ladies would often laugh and coquettishly tease him while offering their help.

"For those of you who didn't register online for the class, I can help you take care of the payment now. Please let me know who didn't register," the chef announced to the class.

Adam raised his hand in the air, and the teacher walked over to him with her credit card reader. While he tried to wipe one hand on the dish towel, he used his other hand to reach for his wallet in his back pocket. His fingers fumbled with the wallet, and it fell from his hand.

"I got it," the teacher said picking up the wallet, which was so full with receipts that it opened in her hand. When she handed it back to him, she looked at Suzy and said, "It's so nice to see a mother and son take a cooking class."

"What? He's not my son!" Suzy exclaimed defensively.

"Oh! I'm so sorry. I just saw that he's about my age and so I thought . . . I'm really sorry." The chef grabbed the credit card from Adam, who stood frozen in place with his hand extended toward the chef.

"He's our age," Suzy said.

"Well, his driver's license says he was born in 1984. I was born in '86. Sometimes we have parents taking classes with their children. That's the only reason I said anything. I'm truly sorry for assuming anything." Adam could tell that the teacher felt embarrassed, and if he hadn't been enduring his own panic attack, he would've felt bad for her. However, in the moment, he desperately wanted her to stop talking.

"I'm not old enough to be his mother," Suzy huffed, placing her hands on her hips. She was clearly infuriated that someone thought she looked old enough to be Adam's mother.

By now the other women surrounded the three of them.

"Well, technically you are old enough to be his mother, if he was born in 1984," Rita said calmly.

Adam was cleaning up his station so he could quickly leave the room. He looked at Rita, but he couldn't tell what she was thinking from her thoughtful demeanor.

"Are you renting the house from your parents?" One of the women asked.

"Yeah, how'd you get to live in this community?" Suzy added.

Adam's initial instinct was to lie, but the truth had already told on itself. He sighed and tossed the kitchen rag on the counter.

"I lied. I wanted to live here so badly that I lied. I'm sorry for deceiving all of you." He wanted to say much more. He wanted to tell them that it was the first time he loved where he was living. He had never engaged with a neighbor, much less gotten to know them by name. Yet, when he looked at their blank facial expressions, he immediately closed up. Without another word, he walked out of the room and went home.

The next morning, Rita paid him a visit. She held out a container of kouigns he had left behind in the kitchen yesterday. Even though it was past nine on a Friday morning, Adam was still in his pajamas. He hadn't slept at all during the night. The incident in last night's cooking class was going to unleash a series of consequences, and he wasn't ready to face them.

"May I come in?" Rita finally asked.

"I'm really sorry for not being honest with all of you," Adam said as he put the kouigns in the refrigerator.

Rita waved her hand. "Please. There are worse neighbors out there. I'm not mad at you, Adam, but this isn't a place for you."

"I don't think I belong out there. I never felt like I fit in with my generation," Adam said.

Rita sat down on his couch and patted the cushion next to her, bidding Adam to sit down. As though he were her child, he sat down and looked at her.

"This community is full of people old enough to be your parents. They're in a different phase of their life. You *are* different, but that doesn't mean you're alone. There are other people out there just like you. Besides, if you didn't get out of here soon, I think Suzy would actually ensnare you. She certainly had her eye on you."

A shiver went down his spine at the thought. "I guess you're right, but I'm going to miss this place very much." Maybe he didn't belong in this community, but he was going to miss the friendships and connections that he had with his neighbors. He doubted he would ever find that same sense of community elsewhere, but he knew that he couldn't always pretend to be someone he wasn't.

"There's a big world out there. You have time to find a place you like. They're not going to kick you out tomorrow. Just keep an open mind. You might surprise yourself." Rita patted his knee and stood up to leave.

"By the way, did you ever suspect that I wasn't old enough?" Adam asked.

"No. I thought you were a pretty convincing middle-aged man," Rita said without any hesitation.

"Oh." He instinctively ran his hand through his hair. He looked forward to returning to his old—or rather—*real* self.

A letter and several calls from the HOA quickly followed. Adam promised that he would be out of the house by the end of the month. To his surprise, Hannah came to his rescue and helped him find a place that was in a quiet neighborhood. She even helped him pack and sat with him when he needed to vent.

A week before his move, Adam finally allowed his parents to see the house that inspired their son to create an alter ego. His mother fell in love with the community, but his father remained unimpressed.

"You're a strange kid," Adam's father said, standing at the kitchen counter. He ran his hand over the granite countertop. "Though I have to say this is a nice kitchen. The materials look like they're good quality, but you don't need to worry about kitchens, Adam. You hate to cook."

"I think this place is gorgeous. I wouldn't mind living here. It's like a health spa," Adam's mother said while she admired the master bathroom, which was mostly packed now. "We should be the ones living here, George!"

George raised his eyebrows skeptically and looked at Adam as if to say, "See what you created?"

On the day of the move, while the movers finished putting all of Adam's furniture and boxes into the truck, a car drove into Rita's driveway. Julia got out of the car and looked over in his direction. He had not seen her since her father had been admitted to the hospital. Now that the truth was out, he didn't feel comfortable talking to anyone from the community. He suffered strange conflicting feelings of shame and loss.

When the moving truck took off for his new residence, Adam walked through the house one more time to make sure nothing had been left behind.

As he was locking the front door, he felt someone watching him. Julia was leaning against his car, her hands tucked in her jean pockets, and she had her usual sarcastic expression.

"You know, a lot of the husbands are relieved that the resident IT guy is moving. I guess you made them feel a little insecure," Julia smiled.

"It's the first time in my life I've ever been popular with the ladies," Adam joked.

Julia laughed. "Well, now that I know you're not some creepy old man, I was going to ask if you want to meet for coffee sometime. Maybe reacclimate to hanging out with people your own age."

Adam was shocked, but he agreed. As soon as they exchanged phone numbers, she unceremoniously walked back to her parents' house.

"Cool. Catch you later," she said.

Even if his stay at Golden Heights was short-lived, Adam had changed. Rita, Mrs. Ryden, and even Suzy pulled him out of his comfort zone, which was always about avoiding people. He felt a little less closed off from the world. No matter what happened to him now, Adam felt he would always be able to deal with it. But he still hoped he would have a reason to come back to Golden Heights, even if just to visit or help one of the residents with their computer issue.

Adam smiled to himself and felt grateful as he walked into Walgreens to buy hair dye to go back to his natural color, whatever it was now.

# THE LOVETTS

The walls of the dining room were burgundy, sparsely decorated with thickly framed oil paintings of bucolic scenescapes. Four place settings were arranged on the long, rectangular table, laden with tall, white candles. The hostess was the first to enter the room, her guests and eventually her husband trailing behind her. She moved like a ballerina: slender, muscular legs walking swiftly, but her torso remaining still. Her arms floated by her side, occasionally wrapping around another person's body or coiling through someone's arm. She spent an equal amount of time displaying affection to each person. Her facial expression was somewhere between gregarious and flirty. The tanned skin on her face was taut, stretched across the geography of her features. When she smiled, her mouth opened broadly, but the rest of her face was unmoved.

The guest with a nearly identical face, but with straight, black hair was the only one not smiling. She kept her arms folded over her chest, pushing her lips forward in a pout. When she thought no one was looking, her gaze shifted toward the hostess's husband, who had sat down at the table and poured himself a glass of red wine. He did not notice the woman's attention on him, and he only looked up from the table when the only other man in the room spoke to him.

"Sam!" The elderly man's heart jumped, and he quickly put his binoculars on the tray beside him. His wife's voice was shrill, a sign that she was looking for trouble. "Did you remember to take your pills? You're up to two a day, remember?" Sabrina put her hands on her hips. "Why is it so dark—you're not spying on the neighbors again, are you?"

"I just wanted to see how effective these binoculars are." He picked up the binoculars. "Oh, look. There's the Big Dipper."

"Don't insult my intelligence. I was born at night, not last night."

"All right, I was watching the Lovetts. They're having a dinner party tonight," he stated matter-of-factly.

"I bought this for you because you enjoyed bird watching. You can't be spying on our neighbors. It's not right," Sabrina argued.

"I'm a dying man. What does it matter?"

"Don't say that, Sam." Sabrina's stern face fell.

The sadness in her eyes was almost too much for him to bear. He was about to say something, when she quickly collected herself.

"Did you see that woman with the black hair? I think she's either having or wants to have an affair with the husband," Sabrina huffed.

Sam held the binoculars toward her. She hesitated at first, but as he expected, Sabrina demurely plucked the instrument from his hand because she enjoyed a good story as much as the next person.

"I can't believe I'm doing this," Sabrina said, holding the binoculars flush against her face. Her hair, a spectrum of brown and gray, cascaded off her back.

"I do gaze at the sky, but sometimes something will catch my attention," he said more to himself, because Sabrina wasn't paying attention.

"She should really lay off the Botox." Sabrina leaned a little closer to the window. "Oh my God! They have that table I wanted. The table in the Restoration Hardware catalog that you thought would look out of place here."

"I *remember*. But we don't even use the dining room. It's become more like your office," he sighed. He was no longer interested in the Lovetts, now that he had to share them with his wife. The few hours after dinner, he came in his office to do work or sometimes just to be alone. He wasn't looking to spy on other people's intimate moments; he just wanted to see how others lived. He had always enjoyed observing people's behavior.

He took a seat behind his desk, pretending to work on the computer. His fingers rested on the keyboard, but he didn't know what he wanted to type. His desk, which used to be cluttered with papers and medical journals, was now completely bare. The polished wood surface was glossy, devoid of the usual coffee stain rings and other signs of himself.

Sabrina kneeled on the couch to get even closer to the window. "She seriously can't move her face! But I do love her skirt. I could never wear a pencil skirt. You have to be a tooth-pick." Sabrina pulled herself away from the binoculars, her expression changing from envy to sadness when she saw Sam's face. Her hands, strong from her years being an equine veterinarian, massaged his shoulders. "Remember when we used to be like them? Of course, we weren't that fancy because we didn't have money at the time, but we used to go up to Flagstaff a couple times a month with Ray and his wife Linda. During the winter, you two would go skiing for hours. You loved that. Maybe we should go up north more often and get out of the heat."

"I can't ski anymore, and I don't see how going up north is going to help matters," he replied tersely.

Though he couldn't see her face at the moment, he imagined her disappointment. She was trying her best to make him feel comfortable, but there was very little she or anyone else could do for him. Seeping through from the living room, jazz music added a heaviness to the air that Sam couldn't describe. He imagined the sounds painted what he no longer had the vocabulary to express.

"I don't know what to do with myself," he muttered, feeling both helpless and irritated that Sabrina was intruding on the one activity he got to enjoy privately.

A year ago, he wouldn't have even had the time to leisurely sit in his office. He was Dr. Samuel Gilden, a practicing psychiatrist for thirty-five years. Some of his therapies were unique, and he received recognition for his work.

After 9/11, he held workshops to help fire fighters, police officers, and volunteers who suffered from PTSD. Most men approaching sixty would have found the full-time work of helping people with their emotional turmoil exhausting. Yet, Sam thrived. It didn't even matter that his time with his wife was limited. He could never imagine himself retiring or cutting back because he truly loved his work. He had never discovered anything else that meant as much to him.

So when the symptoms first emerged, change in mood and forgetting the names of his patients' medications, he chose to ignore them. They were subtle enough that he thought they might turn out to be nothing. However, he was wrong. He began to lose the ability to keep track of his life. Then one evening coming home from his office, he suddenly realized that he couldn't remember how to get home. He pulled off to the side of the road, panic shuddering through his body. He struggled with his cell phone to call Sabrina.

Even though he anticipated the worst, he was still in shock when he was diagnosed with the early stages of Alzheimer's.

"I know this is hard for you, Sam. It's hard for both of us," Sabrina said.

"It may not be quick. I could go on for years lying in bed, slowly deteriorating."

"No!" Sabrina walked over to the other side of the room where his wall was covered with his certificates and family photos. No matter how upset she could get, her pragmatic streak was a thin barrier that always kept her from completely giving way to her emotions. She had an incredible ability to keep her emotions just below the surface.

"We're not there, yet. Far from it," Sabrina said more calmly. "Let's not get ahead of ourselves.

"Please, Sabrina," he begged. "I'm only asking that when there's no quality of life left that you won't make me suffer."

"You're being unfair! What do you want me to do? Smother you with a pillow?"

"No . . ."

Sabrina's eyelids fluttered, her hands wiping her face before the tears had a chance to fall down her cheeks.

Sam rubbed the bridge of his nose. "Remember that really strange movie we saw when we were first dating? It took place in the future, and there were all those people sleeping on the stairs because of overpopulation. It had . . . oh, what's his face? I can picture him–" Sam tapped his forehead, trying desperately to recall the name of the actor.

"Oh!" Sabrina snapped her fingers a couple of times also trying to remember, which momentarily made Sam feel better. "Edward G. Robinson! *Soylent Green*! Now I remember. That was certainly an uplifting movie for date night."

"Remember when the old man went to the ferryman, and he got to see a film of what the earth was like before it was destroyed by humans. How peaceful he was before they let him leave this earth."

"You're not one of the horses that I treat," she said sternly.

"I'm just trying to say that you'll know what to do when the time comes. I need to believe that," he said gently.

Sabrina sat down across from his desk and reached for his hand. Her warm hands enveloped his, and her gray-blue eyes stared right back into this gaze. He felt Sabrina understood, even if it was hard for her to accept that reality now.

"I will always have your back, Sam. I just want us to appreciate the time that we have together," she said.

Sam leaned back in his chair. "The ferryman," he thought to himself. "It was so peaceful."

Suddenly both of them reached for Sam's binoculars. Sabrina lifted them up and gave them to Sam.

The following night Sam looked down at his tray and saw that there were two pairs of binoculars. He looked up at Sabrina and smiled.

"You know how much I love you, Sam. Let's just enjoy now." She handed him his binoculars and slowly reached for hers.

# GUNSMOKE

I tried to focus on different objects in the room, like the family portrait that hung above the television set or the dozens of porcelain dolls that crowded the bookshelves. But my eyes kept shifting toward her colostomy bag peeking through her blouse. I was surprised that she didn't wear a bigger shirt to hide it. Then again, when you're ninety-three years old, maybe you don't care so much.

There was a smell in her place, which I could only describe as the smell of age—a mixture of talcum powder, sour body odor, and potent perfume. I wrung my hands, trying to think of something to say or think to distract my attention from her colostomy bag. My gaze moved toward her hand resting on her belly. The skin hung in papery folds on her thin arms. Thick blue veins wound from her upper forearms to her delicate fingers. But her nails were immaculate. They were long and manicured.

"Your nails are beautiful," I said.

Anne held her hand up to her face. "The nurse offered to paint them for me. It was really nice of her. I'm too shaky to do my own anymore, but I used to keep my nails polished all the time." Anne smiled warmly at me and asked, "Were you born in Phoenix?"

I shook my head, and Anne continued.

"I lived in Oklahoma until 1946 before I moved to Phoenix. When I was really young, my parents had a sizeable ranch house in Oklahoma. This was during the Dust Bowl years. I sure do remember standing beneath those pine trees outside my house and watching the dust fall like it was raining flour. My mother would make me and my brothers stay indoors when the dust got real bad."

I found myself looking at the bag again. She moved just enough so I could really see it this time. Her voice faded in my mind. The bag looked as though it were glued or taped to the side of her stomach. An acidic taste developed in the back of my throat. I swallowed hard, wiggling in my seat. But I couldn't stop looking at it. I felt ashamed.

"Well, I guess I should start your laundry." I rose from my seat.

"Oh. If you don't mind. You don't know how much I appreciate your help. I just don't have the strength anymore."

The pathway to the laundry room was narrow and uneven. I tripped on one of the cobblestones and scraped my elbow against the wall. I took several deep breaths, reminding myself to slow down.

The laundry room, situated toward the back of the complex, was as humid as a sauna. I snapped on my latex gloves. Trying not to look at the dirt accumulating in the floorboards and walls, I dumped the pile of clothes into the washing machine and turned the knob to start the cycle.

Anne did not want me leaving the room while her clothes were in the machine, so I hoisted myself onto the counter and grabbed my book. Sweat droplets congregated across my nose and cheeks. I tried to read, but the oppressive heat sapped my concentration.

When it was time to put her clothes in the dryer, a thin, older woman—not as old as Anne—came into the room. Her arms were holding a round, plastic basket filled with wet clothes. Her blue eyes settled on me as soon as she came in the room.

"Excuse me. Do you know which ones are being used?" Her voice sounded soft and light.

"I think these three are still available," I pointed.

"I wash my clothes in the bathtub. I don't trust the cleanliness of these washing machines, but I have to use the dryers to get my clothes dry. Do you live here?"

"No. I'm a hospice volunteer. I'm taking care of a resident here," I said, making sure not to mention Anne's name. Even volunteers had to follow the confidentiality agreement, and I wanted to protect Anne's privacy.

"I really don't like this complex at all. It's just so dirty, and some of the neighbors can be so grouchy. That's what I get for moving into such a place. The appliances are poor quality. You know every day there's bird poop outside my apartment. In fact, I had to put a note on my door to remind myself not to step in shit. I'm thinking that I'm going to move when my lease is up. By the way, my name is Leslie." She held out her hand. Her handshake was delicate.

"I'm Carrie," I said.

The woman nodded and went back to talking about her noisy neighbors. When the dry cycle was finished, I gathered my things.

"See you around, Carrie."

"Yeah. You take care."

I sat down on one of the benches outside and used my sleeve to wipe the sweat off my face. I was overwhelmed.

Three months ago, I had seen a sign. No, really. Near my house was a billboard advertising the largest hospice in the county. They were looking for volunteers. I drove past this sign a dozen times before I wrote the number on my hand.

"Why do you want to be a hospice volunteer?" the volunteer coordinator had asked me when I signed up for classes.

"Because no one should die alone," I answered, but I also wanted to do this for myself. There was a feeling of fulfillment in knowing that I was capable of making other people's lives a little brighter.

I spent six weeks taking classes, learning about various illnesses like Alzheimer's and cancer, learning the symptoms of each disease and how they progress. I learned what it felt like to be "actively dying," as the hospice liked to refer to this phase in a person's life. I was not disturbed by all that I learned. Yet, here I was, squeamish at the sight of Anne's colostomy bag, which made me feel guilty. My job was to help her, but I learned it was more difficult to watch someone die than I could ever imagine.

When I let myself in, I saw Anne's chin resting on her chest. An episode of *Gunsmoke* was blaring on the television set. Anne's white hair covered her face. I stood in front of her, still holding her sack of laundry. Her billowy blouse made it difficult for me to see if she was breathing.

*Please don't be dead. I can't deal with that right now. Not today. Please don't be dead.*

"Anne," I whispered at first. I said her name a few times, my voice increasingly getting louder. I could feel my heart pounding hard.

Her head popped up after the fourth try. "My show! I must've fallen asleep just before it started. I started watching *Gunsmoke* when I was still a young woman. That Marshall

Dillon was the best. He loved that Miss Kitty," Anne reminisced.

I dropped the sack of clothes and sat down on the chair across from her.

"Of course, dear. Have a seat and rest a while. Don't strain yourself." She took a sip of her coffee, her eyes fixated on the TV. "Watch Marshall Dillon."

I could only nod. I waited for my pulse to return to normal before I started putting her clothes away. During the commercial break, I grabbed the vacuum and started cleaning the living room.

"I have to go to the lab tomorrow," she said, raising her voice so that I could hear her. She squeezed her eyes shut, her head shaking.

"You mean they're drawing blood?" I asked. "I hate needles too."

Her terrified blue eyes reminded me of a child's face. My arms throbbed as I looked at her emaciated arms.

"I haven't had my walk yet. If you're not too tired . . . "

"Of course I'll walk with you!" I sounded more excited than she did.

I helped move her from the couch to the walker. I was terrified that even my grip would cause her delicate skin to bruise, so I lightly placed my hands beneath her upper arms. Her gait was unsteady, so I walked close to her in case she stumbled or needed my assistance. We only walked the length of the parking lot outside the complex because she got tired easily. She paused periodically to admire the different models and colors of cars. She missed driving the most, she said. She repeated this every time we went on our walk.

I heard the sound of flip-flops on the pavement and turned to see Leslie walking toward us. Her tan, athletic legs moved quickly.

"Hello, Anne. It's good to see you up and about," she said a little too loudly, as though she thought Anne might be hard of hearing.

"I'm doing my daily walk. I can't just sit on the couch all day, otherwise I start getting weak," Anne explained. "And Carrie is so sweet to keep me company."

Leslie looked at us, smiling.

"Well, I'm off to go see my little grandbaby. She turns two tomorrow. Enjoy your walk." Leslie walked off toward a red sedan, one of the cars that Anne had admired.

"Is there anything else you need, Anne?" I said when we got back to the apartment.

"You've helped me so much. God bless you." She struggled getting to her feet so she could hug me.

"Thank *you*." I meant it more than I could express to her.

Over the several months I cared for Anne, I felt myself becoming attached to our visits and routine: laundry, vacuuming, watching *Gunsmoke*, and walking around the parking lot. Even *Gunsmoke* had become a regular show in my life. Anne was right. Marshall Dillon really did love Miss Kitty.

"Do you know how to cook?" She asked me one day when I returned with the laundry.

"Not really well," I laughed. "My mother had tried teaching me, but I was better at cleaning up."

"When my husband was still alive, we owned a restaurant and bar. Our food was good, but our drinks were even better because I made them." She winked. "I believed that if you didn't scrimp on the alcohol, people would be satisfied with less and then want to come back because they didn't have to spend a lot of money to have a good time. Mind you, I didn't use too much. Just the right amount. My specialty was Cadillac Margaritas with Gran Gala. Mmm. I used to make those for myself sometimes when we were closing." She smacked her lips, smiling broadly as she remembered.

"Are you ready for your walk today?" I asked after finishing the vacuuming.

"I'm just too tired today. I need to rest."

I nodded, then found myself looking closely at her thin face and the dark circles under her eyes. When I left, she waved from the couch. I waved back, standing there a little too long.

We stopped going for our walks after that visit. Most of the time she sat in front of the television, hovering between sleep and consciousness. Sometimes she experienced surges of energy, and then she would tell me more stories about her past.

"My brother Joey and I used to play bluegrass music. It was about the only time we got along. Our father was a musician, and he got us started real young." She pointed at a banjo propped against the wall. "I played and sang. Joey was wonderful with any string instrument. He could play the guitar, fiddle, even the upright bass. We mostly performed small shows. There was a time when he and I would go up to Flagstaff every weekend to play at The Lounge. The place was beautiful, like a saloon from an old western film." She smiled at the thought.

She ran her finger along the rim of her mug. Her face darkened. "We stopped playing when Joey had his stroke. He lost the use of his right arm, even after all the therapy. He just wasn't the same after that. Nope. He died about five years ago. He was such a talented performer. He really was. I sure do miss him."

I nodded. I never knew how to respond when Anne talked about the death of her loved ones or when she alluded to her own fragility. As her volunteer I was supposed to maintain the proper boundaries. I was not supposed to commiserate with Anne or try to fix her problems, but I truly did feel for her.

The following week I knocked on her screen door and heard her voice, which sounded tired to me. "Come in. The door is unlocked."

She was sitting on the couch, surrounded by magazines, mail, used tissues, and knitted shawls. She was still in her pajamas. Her mouth was fixed in a frown, and her eyes were half closed. I grabbed the laundry and told her I would be back soon.

"How was your weekend?" I asked when I had returned from the laundry room.

"Quiet. Saw my daughter on Sunday."

"That sounds nice. It's good that you have some family near you."

I continued folding the laundry.

"Anne? . . . Hey, I think I should try using a fabric softener for the laundry next time."

My hands rested on the pile of clothes. Next to her bed was a photograph that I had never noticed before. She looked significantly younger. Her hair was a dark color and her face was fuller. She was flanked by two children wearing birthday hats and holding balloons.

"Anne?"

I turned to look at her. Her head was bowed. Even before I checked for a pulse, I had the feeling that she was gone. I grabbed my phone and called the hospice center.

"Does she have a Do Not Resuscitate form?"

"Uh-uh, yes."

"Okay. We're going to send someone over there right now. Can you stay until we get there? Are you all right?"

"Mm-hmm."

"Are you sure?"

"Yes." My arms were trembling now. "I'll stay. I can be here with her as long as you need me."

I sat across from Anne while I waited. Her hands were resting at her side, as though they slid off her lap when she took her last breath. The television was still on, and *Gunsmoke* had just started playing. I turned to look at her, half expecting her eyes to open.

I nearly ran into Leslie on my way to the car. I brushed my fingertips beneath my eyes a few times, always keeping my eyes averted from hers.

"I haven't seen Anne on her walks," Leslie said. She was hugging a grocery bag.

"No," my voice wavered. "The heat has made her tired."

She pulled her sunglasses off her face, "Is everything all right?"

"Sh-she passed away this afternoon." I could barely get the words out of my mouth.

She shook her head, shifting her bag to one arm, "I'm so sorry to hear that. She was a sweet lady. I think it's so wonderful what you're doing. We need more people like you."

"I hope I helped. I really liked Anne."

"Of course you helped. All we old ladies want is a little company. Someone to talk to."

All attempts to appear calm failed. I pretended to rub my eyes from exhaustion. Leslie put her hand on top of mine.

"It's okay." She smiled gently and squeezed my hand.

"I—I didn't know her that long. I'm not supposed to cry."

"You're human, honey. Dying is a pain and death is a bitch. You wouldn't be normal if it didn't get to you in some way."

She patted me gently on the shoulder, and then I watched her walk back to her apartment.

I sat down on the bench in the courtyard of the complex, feeling empty inside. I would never again drive to this apartment complex. Even though the buildings were old and showing wear, I thought that I would actually miss this place a little because it reminded me of Anne, and now I wondered if I could or would feel this bond with the next person the hospice assigned to me.

It was hard to believe that just a few hours ago I was talking to Anne. Now she was gone. Of course I knew people that had passed away, but I had never actually seen it. Life suddenly felt more fragile to me and also more precious.

I stood up and brushed the dust off my backside. I felt strongly that I would continue to do this kind of work. I would never forget my time with Anne. Some things stay in your mind for a lifetime. This, I thought, would be one of them.

# WHERE THE ANIMALS ROAM

## Kingman, Arizona 1978

S itting in his car, Police Officer Tom Mittle plucked the toothpick from between his lips to scrape the dirt beneath his thumbnail. He nearly pricked his finger when a blue 1967 Dodge Dart whizzed down the road. Mittle's radar gun recorded the vehicle going seventy-eight miles per hour. It was not uncommon for drivers to speed down the highway since it was just open road for miles. Mittle shook his head as he switched on the sirens. Sometimes he felt badly for the people traveling through the area. It certainly was tempting for people to speed, but his job was to enforce the law.

The driver of the Dart slowed down and pulled over to the side of the road. Mittle sauntered toward the vehicle, his paunch swaying over his tightly belted pants.

"What seems to be the problem, officer?" the driver asked, flashing a charming smile with perfectly straight, bright white teeth.

Mittle paused for a moment, scrutinizing the young man's handsome face and nice-looking, dark blue suit. The driver's gaze repeatedly shifted toward the rearview mirror. A bandage covered a wound above his left eye, and the left sleeve of his jacket was torn at the forearm.

"Everything all right, son? Looks like you've had a rough time," Mittle asked.

"Oh, it's nothing. Just a clumsy accident," the driver answered, sounding slightly uncertain.

"Do you know how fast you were going?" Mittle asked.

"No, officer."

"You were going seventy-eight in a fifty-five mile-per-hour zone. I'm going to need your license and registration."

Mittle took the items from the driver and went back to his car to write up a ticket. Handing the ticket to the driver, Mittle took another close look at him. He could see a little bit of the wound peeking beyond the edge of the bandage.

"Welcome to Kingman, Harry Denning," he said, returning to his car to wait for the next stranger to pass through the small town.

\* \* \*

Later that day, Harry rented a small and unobtrusive trailer. Now, he wanted to be as inconspicuous as his trailer, but Officer Mittle hadn't been the only person to notice Harry Denning's arrival. Kingman was a small town, so Harry wasn't too surprised that many of its residents were suspicious of him. The fact was the only people who could possibly know him were the few individuals he had sold marijuana and cocaine to sometime in the past. Harry was, or had been, a runner for a drug operation that ran from Mexico to Las Vegas. Kingman was one of the stopping points where Harry and his former partner, Robby, had done business, but they never stayed long and they kept a very low profile.

Over a short period of time, the people paid Harry less attention. Only Mrs. Johnson, the owner of Holly's Diner, took notice of him, since she thought he looked like Ricky Nelson from *The Ozzy and Harriet Show*.

When he wasn't reading the local newspaper, he paced the inside of the trailer. His injured leg was beginning to hurt more. Every hour, he peeked through the curtains, desperately praying that he wouldn't see a black Cadillac Eldorado pulling in front of his place. Yet with every minute that passed, he felt a moment closer to confronting the inevitable.

Harry walked over to the map he had spread out on the little square kitchen table. His index finger tapped the areas where he had heard there were tunnels. He tried to imagine where Robby might have hidden the money. He had to find that money.

Robby had been Harry's friend, or so he thought. They frequently worked together transporting drugs through Kingman. Both of them made a lot of money for two men in their midtwenties. They had a good thing going for a while, until Robby admitted to Harry that he had skimmed some of the money for several months and was hiding it in a tunnel somewhere in Kingman. Harry had been horrified. The men who worked in this line of business were ruthless and brutal. If Robby was in trouble, then so was Harry.

That night Harry discovered Robby and his entire family butchered in their home. Harry was in the midst of packing his belongings to get out of town when two men carrying assault rifles broke into his apartment.

Harry narrowly escaped through a tiny square window in his bathroom. They had punched a hole in the bathroom door, just before Harry made the twenty-foot drop from the bathroom window. The left side of his body took the brunt of the fall, and a sharp pain seared through his lower leg as he ran toward his car.

Still intently staring at the map, Harry grabbed the bottle of whiskey and drank two large swigs. He wiped the beads of sweat on his upper lip with the back of his hand.

He was running out of time. He needed to find that money soon so he could return what Robby stole and hopefully save his own life. His chances were slim and the money was a needle in a barn full of hay, but Harry was used to fighting against the odds until there was nothing left to lose.

Early in the morning, just as soon as the sun was peeking above the horizon, he drove on the long stretches of asphalt passing through the town and then the dirt roads meandering further into the unpopulated desert. Every particular land-scape and areas of soft ground he marked on a map flattened against the passenger seat. He discovered an abandoned tunnel roughly twenty feet away from a dirt road that connected to Route 66. The entrance was mostly covered by mesquite trees and planks of wood. If he hadn't been searching for these types of landmarks, he wouldn't have even noticed the entrance to the tunnel.

Standing in front of the tunnel with one hand on his hip and the other shielding his eyes from the sun, Harry looked around to make sure he was alone. Gripping the flashlight, he carefully lifted one leg and then the other over the planks. The narrow beam of light was barely strong enough to illuminate the narrow pathway. He stood in the same place, moving the flashlight slowly, but all he could see was dirt and a narrow path that curved slightly to the right. When he tried to move forward, it was as if his body rebelled. He felt frozen. His injured leg started to throb. His breath immediately quickened, and for a moment, he thought he was suffocating until he remembered he was only several feet away from the entrance.

Steeling his resolve, Harry continued walking down the tunnel, sweeping the beam of light back and forth. He saw graffiti and trash littering the pathway. When he looked behind him, the light from the tunnel seemed so far away. Just as he felt like he couldn't go any further, he found the end of the tunnel. There was an empty, large steel container. He examined the container, but there was no sign of the money.

His insides felt like they were liquifying, and he quickly stumbled toward the light from the entrance. His bad leg got caught on the beams, and he fell on the rocky surface, cutting up his palms and forearms. Back in his car, he marked the site on the map. He crossed off the spot several times, the pressure from the ballpoint pen tearing through the paper.

He spent the rest of the day looking for more tunnels, but his search was unsuccessful. On his way home he saw a yellow neon sign that read Barking Nuggets Brewery. At the moment, the idea of sitting somewhere in public made him feel safer. Even though he wasn't in the mood to drink, he parked his car between the cluster of motorcycles.

The outside of the building looked more like an abandoned shack than a proper bar. A dozen or so motorcycles were parked outside the establishment. Harry's eyes slowly adjusted to the dimly lit room as he sat down at the bar, admiring the young woman behind the counter. She wore bell bottoms and a Rolling Stones T-shirt. Her bleached blond hair was perfectly straight and parted in the middle, and her green eyes were thickly lined in black eyeliner and long, false eyelashes.

When she caught him staring at her, she slapped a napkin on the counter, inches away from his hand. Forcing himself to smile, he ordered a beer.

"You must be new here. I've been living here too long not to recognize a face," she said. "I'm Layla."

"Nice to meet you, Layla. You're right. I am new here. I'm from Vegas." Harry intentionally avoided telling her his name. He didn't want anyone to be potentially dragged into his mess.

She laughed. "We're like the polar opposite of Vegas. We're a small town with not very much to do." Layla set down his drink. "So why Kingman, anyways?"

Harry shrugged. "It seemed as good a place as any. I grew up in Casa Grande, so I'm used to small towns."

"Well, I'd do almost anything to get out of this small town. I've been here my whole life." Layla picked up an empty glass someone left at the bar and emptied an ash tray.

"A friend of mine told me how Kingman is sitting on a web of tunnels. Is that true?" Harry tried to sound nonchalant, but his usual charm with women was lacking tonight.

She crossed her arms over her chest, one eyebrow lifting. "Sure, there's some tunnels out there, but it's not like you're gonna find buried treasure. Most of the tunnels have been abandoned for years. But, if you're that interested in tunnels, you should go talk to Red. He's been working in the mines for years. He would know something about tunnels."

Layla nodded toward the pool table and then left to take care of the other patrons. Harry watched a group of men hovering around the pool table. In the center of the group, was a man with a muscular, stocky build and a face framed with rusty-red hair. That must be Red, Harry thought. Red stretched his arms wide and raised his voice to be heard over the house music. He was trying to persuade one of the guys to play for money.

"I'll play. What are you betting?" Harry moved in front of the other men.

"All right, pretty boy." The red-haired man smiled, his

toughened skin crinkling into a web of lines around his eyes and mouth.

Both men handed a five-dollar bill to the bartender to hold onto while they played.

Despite the fact that the pool table was worn and uneven, Harry still managed to play well. He never told anyone that his father had taught him to play pool when he was a teenager. His father was an expert billiard player who spent the weekends at bars and pool halls making bets with the other players. Most of the time, his father was successful, bringing home more money than he made in a week working as a diesel mechanic. But when his father lost, Harry and his mother kept their distance. A veil of bleakness persisted until the next time his father won at pool. As Harry got older, he watched his father compete against many men. He learned by watching and listening. Anytime Harry saw a shot that impressed him, he practiced that move until he had perfected it. He was passionate about the game, and he fell in love with the excitement of betting.

Throughout the game, Harry and the red-haired man enjoyed friendly bantering and competition. Harry's opponent said that his real name was Melvin Thompson, but everyone called him Red. He had settled down in Kingman after working several years on the Santa Fe Railroad.

"I've been living here for nearly twenty-five years." Red leaned real low against the pool table, carefully aligning his shot. "Young men like you don't just show up here to put down roots."

Harry watched the white ball bounce against the table and lightly tap the red striped ball into the pocket. Red was a better player than Harry thought he would be.

"Layla told me you knew a lot about tunnels," Harry said flatly, missing the shot. He had lost his focus on the game. "A buddy of mine had some kind of obsession with these rumored tunnels you have here in town. Made me curious."

"Why? Most of them have been abandoned for years. You couldn't pay me enough to go inside one of those old tunnels." Red walked around the table assessing his final shot.

After a while, Harry began to think that nothing more would come from the conversation. He let out a low, long whistle when Red made the winning shot. Even though it was a friendly game, he still hated defeat.

"Good game," Red said, collecting his money from Layla and stuffing the bill into his wallet. "I'll tell you what. Duval is always looking for workers, and I could use more people right now. I lost three men last week.

"What happened to those guys?" Harry asked, his eyes widening.

Red laughed, "Relax. People come and go in this town. As long as you can move dirt, we'll put you to work."

"But I don't need a job," Harry said. Truthfully, he knew he could really use the money. The amount that he had left would only last him another week or two at most. And yet at this point, he wasn't sure he'd live long enough to actually run out of money.

"If you can help me out at Duval, I'll tell you everything I know about the tunnels in this town." Red promised.

"Deal." Harry extended his hand, which Red shook firmly.

Harry ordered another beer at the bar and took a seat where he wouldn't draw attention to himself. He kept glancing down at the floor, wondering if there was some tunnel passing beneath the building's foundation. He didn't want to learn anything more about these tunnels at this moment. The thought of going into another one suddenly made him feel claustrophobic and nauseated. But he wanted to live, and the fear of being killed was enough to continue pushing him forward.

When Layla was looking away from Harry's direction, he slowly got up from his chair. His injured leg was throbbing badly. Harry didn't want anyone to know that he was injured. He didn't believe in showing vulnerability. Clenching his teeth, Harry limped toward the door. He glanced back one more time toward the counter. Layla looked up, just long enough to wink at him.

* * *

The Duval facility was a series of concrete rectangular structures. The interior was just as dull, with bare, gray walls, bluish-gray curtains, and yellow plastic chairs. When Harry found the HR department, a hefty-looking woman, with graying hair tied in a loose bun on the top of her head, handed him an application. He sat uncomfortably in a school desk, filling out the paperwork. When he returned the completed application, the woman adjusted her thick, pink-framed glasses, looking at him as though she had just seen him for the first time. Harry straightened his posture, suddenly feeling self-consciousness about his slender frame. After an awkward moment, the woman sighed and dropped his application in a drawer.

A few hours later Harry received news that the company accepted his application. They assigned him four ten-hour shifts, beginning the following day.

He reported to the copper mining site, a forty-five minute drive from his trailer. From his car, the land did not look like a mining site. The surface of the land seemed uninterrupted. Yet, as he walked toward the miners, he saw tracks leading to one of the tunnels. The entrance was supported with wooden beams and planks.

Staring at the entrance, he imagined his body being swallowed by the darkness. He took a deep breath, but it felt as though his lungs couldn't take in the oxygen. Panic tingled in his toes and fingers, and he kept inhaling deeply until his body released a yawn.

"Pretty boy, what are you doing standing around? This ain't a tourist attraction."

Harry felt a hand on his shoulder, and he turned around to see Red wearing a white hard hat and a thick leather belt with several large pouches holding various tools. Before Harry could say anything, Red barked orders to everyone. Today Harry's job was to wheel the dirt from the skip to the entrance of the tunnel.

Trudging behind the workers through the dimly lit tunnel, a rush of cold sweat covered his skin. The ground felt as though it were slipping away from his boots. The path declined quickly as they neared one of the mine cages, which carried Red and the rest of workers to the lower level. When he thought no one was looking, Harry pressed his hand against the wall, feeling the cool, solid earth against his palm. While he waited for the first batch of ore, he listened to the snippets of men's voices amid the hum of pickaxes and machinery. Pushing the cart back and forth, his leg started to ache. He made sure to carry his weight differently to disguise the limp, but everyone seemed too preoccupied to even notice or care. By midday, his entire body ached. The cart was heavy, and he had to push with his whole body just to get it to budge. During their lunch, he sat by himself. Harry hoped that the miners would continue to ignore him as he was in no mood to talk. He hated to be in pain, and he wondered how the other workers, many of them older than him, managed to survive the physical labor.

Red watched Harry for a while before finally walking over to sit with him. He pulled out a sandwich from his lunch box and offered half to Harry, who had forgotten to bring lunch with him. Harry gratefully looked at the bologna between two thin slices of crusty white bread. He was starving and accepted the sandwich.

Red stuffed a corner of the sandwich into his mouth. "Hey, check this out."

He opened his lunch box and removed a handkerchief. Tucked between Snickers wrappers and used napkins, Red pulled out a rock the size of a shot glass. The swirls and blotches of turquoise marked the russet brown chunk of stone.

"When I first started working in the mines, I found this piece and I've kept it with me ever since. We're not supposed to take any turquoise from the premises, but this is my lucky stone." Red rewrapped the stone in the handkerchief and put it back into the box. "I'm always amazed at the beauty that you can find in the dirt."

"How many tunnels are in Kingman?" Harry pressed.

"Who knows. I've heard Kingman underground is like Swiss cheese. Hundreds of tunnels going every which direction. Of course, the city officials won't admit this information. They don't want the people to know because everyone and their sister'll start exploring. It's dangerous. Many of them have been abandoned for years. The most known tunnel is the one beneath the Brunswick Hotel. It connects to a train depot. Back in the day, immigrants used to hide in the tunnels and cross the street underground from the train depot to the hotel." Red pulled out a cigarette and offered one to Harry, but Harry shook his head.

"How do you find them? The tunnels?" Harry asked.

Suddenly, Red pointed off in the distance. "Look over there!"

A large form moved slowly toward them. Its long, spindly legs kicked up the dust. Its tan hide blended with the landscape. Harry squinted, unable to believe what he was seeing. As the animal moved closer, the other men around them stopped what they were doing to watch the camel roaming through the desert.

Red nodded. "About a hundred years ago or so, people brought camels and mules to Kingman to do some of the labor. As Kingman became more of a mining town, they stopped using animals for work and just set them free. Every now and again you'll see one of them wandering," Red said, brushing the dust off his pants.

"I never realized how majestic they are," Harry responded distractedly.

The throbbing in Harry's body increased. When he tried to stand up, the pain in his leg overwhelmed him. Willing his face to not expose anything, he grabbed the chain link fence next to him to keep himself from falling.

"I noticed that limp of yours." Red arched his back, stretching his arms wide.

"It's nothing," Harry lied, rubbing his leg just below the knee cap. He was beginning to worry that his leg would never feel normal again. However, some of this fear was assuaged by his jealousy of Red, who showed no signs of exhaustion. "I don't know how you do it. You're older than I am."

Red laughed boisterously, tilting his head back and patting his flat stomach. "I've been doing work like this since I was fifteen years old. I'm used to it. You'll get used to it too. You're young."

Just a few weeks ago, Harry would have looked at Red and felt sorry for him. Now, he almost envied Red. Harry was a lot like his own father, who was attracted to risk and money. Right now, risk and wealth held no fascination for Harry because every moment that passed was a moment closer to him being found and killed. He was starting to worry that he might not find the money Robby stole.

"Time's not on my side," Harry muttered more to himself than to Red.

"Time isn't on anyone's side. Come on. Lunch break's over," Red replied.

\* \* \*

For the next few days Harry transported the ore out of the tunnel and prepared it to be shipped from Duval to a smelting plant. Though the work was arduous, at times he was able to forget his life was in danger. When the day ended, he was exhausted, his body quivering from pain. He took ibuprofen and sat in an easy chair and tried to read the newspaper. Sometimes when he saw a shadow or movement in his peripheral vision, he jumped, every muscle in his body tightening in anticipation. There was never anything there, but the anxiety continued to pulsate through his body for hours.

He couldn't sleep. Sometimes he spent the entire night staring at the ceiling. His fears were beginning to consume him. During the day, he felt like a dead man walking.

"Must be something really interesting out there." Red approached Harry, who stood gazing at the barren desert landscape. Red removed his hard hat, wiping the sweat dribbling down his forehead.

"I keep looking for that camel. That was quite a sight," Harry said.

"It's pretty rare to see them roaming. I'm sure there aren't too many of them left–Don't move!" Red gripped Harry's arm to keep him still.

"What's wrong?"

"Don't you hear it? You don't ever want one of those to bite you." Red pointed to a rattlesnake coiled near the base of some shrubbery, the tip of its tail vibrating.

"I've never seen one up close," Harry responded, leaning forward slightly, despite Red's firm grip.

"Yeah . . . it's not something to get too excited about either. They don't go looking for trouble. So don't provoke them, or you'll be a dead man."

Harry continued to watch the snake with a combination of awe and terror until it slithered out of sight.

\* \* \*

Thanks to Red, Harry eventually found another tunnel while driving and hiking through Kingman. This particular tunnel was behind an abandoned building. The structure was so dilapidated that he couldn't determine how this tunnel had been used. Equipped with a flashlight and a crowbar, he steadily moved his legs toward the opening of the tunnel. He knew what he was doing was dangerous and reckless, but he felt that he had no choice.

The flashlight's beam illuminated the cavernous tunnel. Harry walked slowly so that he wouldn't trip. The path seemed to continue for a long time and then suddenly it stopped. Wooden boards blocked whatever was on the other side of the tunnel.

Harry turned off his flashlight, immersing himself in the complete darkness. At first, he felt nauseated and claustrophobic. Even though he desperately wanted to turn the flashlight back on, he forced himself to remain still. He loosened his grip on the crowbar until it slipped through his finger, making a thud sound when it bounced on the hard earth. When his breathing slowed, he reopened his eyes. It felt so strange to him to see absolutely nothing, except blackness.

After a while of being fully enveloped in the dark, Harry felt the world become more and more distant. He lost track of time. Even the pain in his leg seemed to disappear. Harry felt like his soul were a balloon that would float upward if it weren't for the string that connected his body to the earth.

When he finally felt ready, he switched the flashlight back on, retrieved the crow bar, and walked out of the tunnel. That night he collapsed onto his bed and immediately fell asleep without having to drink an ounce of alcohol. All he had left was exhaustion.

The next morning, Harry woke up feeling so famished that he drove to Holly's Diner and chose a booth at the back of the restaurant.

"What can I get you, sweetie?" Mrs. Johnson beamed when she got to his table.

Harry ordered eggs, hash browns, and bacon. When Mrs. Johnson brought his coffee, he poured three plastic containers of creamer while thinking about where he would look for more tunnels.

As soon as Mrs. Johnson set down the plate, Harry stuffed his mouth with food. He hadn't felt like eating in days, and now it felt like he was making up for all the meals he'd missed.

"Enjoying your last meal, Handsome Harry?" The voice was low and smooth.

Harry almost choked on his omelet. He never expected to be caught quite like this, with his mouth full of food.

"I was until now." Harry continued to clear his throat and took several gulps of water.

The man sat down in the booth and removed his gold-rimmed aviator sunglasses, revealing a pair of expressionless, pale blue eyes. He shoved a stick of gum into his mouth and carefully folded the silver wrapper into a tiny square, dropping it into Harry's coffee.

"Is there something I can get you?" Mrs. Johnson asked the man.

"Nothing for me. We won't be here long," the man answered calmly.

His name was Jackson "The Grinder" Reed, and he was the cartel boss's right-hand man. It was his job to "eliminate" problems. His nickname "The Grinder" referred to an incident in which he stuffed a man's arm into a meat grinder. Harry hoped that this was only an isolated incident.

Harry simply stared at the lean, sculpted frame, clad in a fitted black polo shirt that emphasized Reed's large biceps. In a dumbfounded manner, Harry pulled out his wallet and left enough cash to provide Mrs. Johnson a very generous tip. He wasn't going to have to worry about money much longer.

"Why don't you just let me keep looking for the money? I promise to give it to you. I never took the money in the first place," Harry blurted.

"It's too late. That money Robby stole belonged to our associates, and they're very angry that their money went missing. They gave their terms for compensation," Reed answered patiently. There was zero emotion in his voice.

The color drained from Harry's face. "I just need a little more time. I promise I won't stop till I find it. I didn't take the money. Why should I die for another man's mistake?"

"You were never cut out for this line of work. In this world, his mistake is your mistake." Reed stood up, and Harry followed him, dragging his feet toward Reed's black Cadillac Eldorado sitting next to his car.

"I never cared much for small towns," Reed said once they

were on one of the main roads leading out of the town. "I like the noise and chaos of Vegas. Kingman is too quiet for my taste."

Harry watched the needle on the speedometer climb until it hovered around eighty. Leaning back against the head rest, he shut his eyes, willing himself to stay calm. When he suddenly heard the wailing sound of sirens, Harry thought he had imagined the noise. He looked over his shoulder to see the blue and red flashing lights.

Reed pulled over too quickly, and Harry felt some whiplash. The brakes moaned, and the car rocked as the tires rolled over the uneven surface.

While rubbing his neck, Harry looked out the window and recognized the mile marker. They were close to the first tunnel he had found when he arrived in Kingman.

As Officer Mittle walked toward them, Harry's mind worked quickly. He now felt a little affection toward the blubbery officer. He just needed a little more time.

"What's the rush, gentlemen?" Mittle said, his face darkening when he recognized Harry. "You again. . ."

Harry took his eyes off Reed to meet Mittle's gaze and mouthed the word "gun." The vinyl seat creaked as Reed's sinewy body shifted just slightly. Mittle's hand swiftly moved toward his holster. Reed's gun was already pointed at Mittle when Harry pulled the pen from his shirt pocket and stabbed Reed in the neck.

A shot rang out, and the ringing sound in his ears disoriented Harry. He jumped out of the car and started running toward the tunnel. He made sure to run in a zig-zag pattern. When one of the bullets barely missed his leg, Harry realized Reed was still following him. His legs felt like rubber and his lungs started burning. Finally, he saw the entrance to the tunnel and he pitched himself forward into the darkness. His ankles rolled awkwardly over the uneven ground, but he kept moving quickly, his arms extended in front of him.

Two sharp, loud cracks rumbled through the tunnel. Before Harry recognized the noise as gunshots, he was overwhelmed with the pain in his side. He stumbled, touching the space just below his ribs. Wetness oozed between his fingers. He tried to keep moving, but the pain overwhelmed him and he tumbled forward. His palms skidded on the dirt, and, for a moment, he felt something metal and rough brush against his skin. Reed caught up to him, his shoe smacking into Harry's forehead.

Harry's head snapped back and for a moment he was completely disoriented. He couldn't see anything in the impenetrable blackness, but he could feel Reed's kicks in the darkness, loudly cursing. Harry patted the dirt around him until his fingertips brushed against the metal again. This time his hand wrapped around the steel bar. He pushed himself off the ground, swinging the rebar toward the sound of Reed's voice. He missed the first time, nearly losing his balance from the momentum. He swung again, this time making contact. Reed grunted once and then he was silent. Harry continued hitting Reed, his screams reverberating in the darkness, until the hardened surface yielded into mush.

Harry dropped to his knees, his fingertips brushing against the bloody mass. By now the throbbing in his leg and his torso almost made him lose his senses. Heat and tingling sensations swept through his entire body. As he crawled around the body, Harry half expected Reed to snatch his leg or ankle. But nothing happened as he continued to crawl down the tunnel. Gradually a blur of whiteness loomed ahead of him, and he started to crawl faster. As he slithered past the shadow's edge into the sunlight, the coppery taste in his mouth bloomed. Saliva dribbled down his lips, and he collapsed onto the ground and grabbed his waist.

Off in the distance he thought he saw a silhouette moving toward him.

"Officer Mittle?" Harry called out weakly. He hoped it was the officer.

Harry's vision began to tunnel. Rolling onto his back, Harry squinted from the brightness of the sun. He thought he saw Red with his smiling, weathered face. Or was it Officer Mittle?

Relief poured out of him in long, heavy breaths. Whatever would happen next was out of his hands.

# AVA

## 1979

"I know I'm right. Fifty million Frenchmen can't be wrong," my mother, Ava, stated as though it were a fact.

I grabbed my three-year-old daughter, Lily, who was running around the living room with her arms out like an airplane. She wriggled in my grasp when I tried to sit her on my lap. Her dark, curly locks were frizzing, making my nose itch.

"Not the fifty million Frenchmen again," I retorted. From the time I was a little girl, my mother would try to win any argument with the fictitious Frenchmen—fifty million of them, no less. As an adult, I learned she picked up this phrase from the 1929 musical comedy called, of course, *Fifty Million Frenchmen*.

Ava got up to get a new pack of cigarettes from her purse and walked to the fridge to grab orange juice and vodka so she could make a screwdriver.

"That husband of yours is irresponsible, and it's going to get you into trouble. Why does he have to leave a company that's paid him good money?" she asked.

"Because they weren't treating him well, and this new business is his passion. Sometimes we have to follow our dreams, Mom." I stood up so that I was not looking up at her, but I would never be able to look her in the eyes. She was six feet tall without heels. "I have to go to the hospital again. Dad can't go home until the test results come back."

Ava slammed her drink on the counter. Orange droplets jumped out of the glass. Lily walked toward the freezer pointing her finger and shaking her head, repeating the word "Pocklepee! Pocklepee!"

"Can she have a popsicle?" I asked.

"You got to see him last week. This is my week." Ava was getting stressed, which was never good.

"He had a heart attack, Mom. A minor one, thank goodness, but I want to make sure he's okay."

"Why can't Dana take care of him? She's his wife now."

"Please, Mom. Don't do this."

Ava waved her hand and went to her bedroom, slamming the door shut.

\* \* \*

Dad had a small room to himself on the fourth floor of the hospital. When I got there, he and Dana were both immersed in their reading. When I gently knocked on the door, which was ajar, both their heads popped up. Dana rushed over to give me a hug and then she immediately picked Lily up in her arms.

"You should have told me you were coming." Dana showered the crown of Lily's head with kisses. "And it's wonderful to see my granddaughter."

"How are you doing, Dad?" I gave him a hug. He grabbed my hand and squeezed it.

"I'm hanging in there. They're supposed to let me out tomorrow."

Dana offered to take Lily to the cafeteria to have some Jell-O. As soon as she left, my guard came down. The tension between my parents always manifested in stomach pain. I felt my face tighten.

"Does Ava know you're here?"

I nodded.

"I don't want you stressing yourself out over this, sweetheart. It's not worth your health."

"Don't be ridiculous. I want to be here with you. I don't know why she gets into such a rage."

"Well," he let out a yawn, "your mother is a character. She's always been that way, and I don't expect that she'll ever change. I think that's the sad and honest truth."

"Did you ever worry that I was going to turn out like her?"

"I never thought about it that way. I loved your mother. I still do, but I couldn't make her happy, and that rage of hers was hard to deal with. I'm sorry you got caught in the middle."

"I just don't want her to be so angry and negative all the time," I said softly. My vision blurred as tears welled up in my eyes.

"I know. But you need to take care of yourself, too. You have a child who needs you." He kissed the top of my hand, patting it gently. "By the way, you two aren't staying with her, are you?"

"No. We're staying at the Sheridan."

"Good. That woman smokes like a fiend. You don't need Lily breathing that in."

I gathered my things slowly, reluctant to leave. I didn't know when I was going to see my dad again. We lived on opposite sides of the country now, and each visit was precious. My father was in his late seventies, and his health was always fragile. There was no guarantee that I would ever see him again.

"Give David my love," he said when I reached the door.

"I will. He wishes he could've come on this trip, but right now the business needs his full attention." I turned and waved, trying my best to smile. "Love you, Daddy."

* * *

A few nights later, just before I was supposed to return to California, Ava asked me to have dinner with her and her friend Milly. Dana and my father, who was home now from the hospital, offered to watch Lily for the night. I bought a bouquet of yellow roses for Milly and a bottle of wine for the three of us.

Milly lived in a brownstone in Central Park East. Her late husband had been a lawyer. When he was still alive, my parents used to play bridge with them almost every weekend. This was before my parents divorced nearly twenty years ago. After the divorce, Milly chose to forgo her friendship with my father so that she could continue being friends with Ava. My mother was successful in painting my father as the bad guy, the "no good bum."

My mother was in one of her better moods that night. Her face looked radiant as she told Milly and I stories about her most recent affair with a taxi driver. I sat quietly, nursing the glass of wine I had been sipping for almost two hours. It was so rare for me to see her happy that I just wanted to appreciate the moment.

"I swear that man can't follow speed limits to save his life. If the music is fast, he drives fast. If the music is slow, he drives slow." Ava rested her elbows on her knees, giving us a look like she had a secret to share. "We almost got kicked off our flight to Las Vegas. I had to use the ladies' room when they started boarding the plane, so he boarded without me so he could get us our seats. Well, when I finally boarded the plane, I saw him, and without even thinking I yelled, 'Hi, Jack!' Everyone jumped two feet in the air because they thought someone hijacked the plane."

"Speaking of getting kicked out," Milly began, "did you know our friend Beth's son was expelled from his university for getting caught with marijuana? Can you imagine? This brilliant boy, who worked so hard to get into school, is now back living with his parents. It must be hard to be that age now. In my day it was alcohol. The drugs still existed, but you never really heard anything about it. But nowadays these kids have a buffet with all these different, new kinds of drugs at their disposal, not to mention the peer pressure that goes with it."

My mother glanced in my direction, "Well, you know it started with the flower children. What one generation accepts, the next embraces. But I'll tell you something, I've tried marijuana–"

"You have?" Milly and I both exclaimed.

"Jack bought some for us a couple of times. He loved it, so I gave it a try. It's all right. But I still don't know what all the fuss is about."

"Didn't you feel *something*?" Milly asked.

"Maybe a little, but I really didn't have that much. I still prefer my Luckys." I noticed the corners of Ava's mouth raised just slightly. It looked like a coy smile to me.

"Have you ever wanted to try pot, Milly?" I was curious. I could immediately feel my mother's attention shift toward me.

Milly ran her hands over her legs, as though she were trying to smooth out the wrinkles in her slacks. She seemed to be looking out, but at nothing in particular.

"I don't know if I've ever given it that much thought. But I guess I wouldn't mind trying it someday."

Milly saw that my mother was still looking at me. She

swiveled in her chair so that she was looking right at my face. "Do you smoke pot?"

I pulled out an old Sucrets tin case and displayed the contents.

"Sheryl Renee Lennox!" My mother said, trying to snatch the tin from my hand.

"Wait just a second, Ava. I have questions." Milly gently persuaded my mother to sit back down. "Do you seriously carry this around with you, Sheryl?"

"I'm not going to take my chances and leave it in the hotel room."

"But how did you get it on the plane?"

"There are ways," was all I was going to say.

"Does Lily—"

"No. Lily has no idea. I wouldn't use it in front of her."

"So, you've been keeping this a secret from everyone?"

"I don't go around advertising this fact about me. I'm almost forty years old. This is who I am, and this is something I enjoy. I don't think that we should criminalize marijuana."

No one said a word. My mother pulled out her next cigarette. I set the tin down and sunk into the sofa cushions. I never intended to share this fact about my life, and I'm not even sure why I bothered. Maybe the conversation about pot gave me a false sense of comfort in sharing this secret of mine. Or perhaps I was willing to be ridiculous if it meant finding something that would make me feel more connected with my mother.

I don't know who brought it up first (I think it was Milly), but they decided that Milly wanted to "try it." From the way Milly handled herself, I wondered if she had been completely honest about this being her first time. They both maintained their composure as though they were trying a new wine. I stifled a chuckle watching them. I had never imagined ever experiencing this moment with my mother. I was smiling at both of them. I loved them both and it was so nice to relax with my mother, the first time this visit.

When my mother lit the joint, the usual feeling of tension that I felt in my body when I was around her began to lift. She had always been a formidable, intimidating figure whose hostility and negativity had overwhelmed me since I was a child. I had survived my years living with her by turning inward, by creating an internal fantasy world where I could escape. Even now, I endured abdominal pain, a manifestation of the stress I internalized. Yet here she was before me, older and more delicate looking. The way that she sat on the couch, her face softening into a peaceful expression, reminded me of how she could have been. It took me almost thirty years to understand that it wasn't my father's or my fault that she was so unhappy and angry. I understood that we would never have the kind of relationship that most mothers and daughters had, and the realization of this often made me feel angry toward her. But now I wanted to share a bond with my mother before it was too late. What if I repeated this history with my own daughter?

"So, is this what you learned in college?" My mother said, her voice tinged in sarcasm.

"After college. I dated an artist named Tommy, who liked to smoke before he went into the studio."

Milly went to her collection of records, pulling one out and putting it on a turntable. I recognized Sammy Davis's voice immediately. Milly sang, her body swaying to the music. My mother started to giggle.

"That song was playing the night your father proposed to me at the Supper Club in Atlantic City," my mother said softly when the music ended.

\* \* \*

I went to my mother's apartment the next morning after dropping Lily off to say goodbye to my dad.

"When will you bring Lily here?" My mother was slamming cabinet doors.

My body erupted in a hot flash. "Our flight leaves in the early afternoon, and I still have to pick her up from Dad's."

"That son of a bitch," she muttered.

My mother was spilling coffee grounds all over the counter, trying to make a pot of a coffee. The cigarette in her mouth was still unlit. Her face looked drawn. She hadn't washed her face, and the makeup was smudged beneath her eyes and cheeks.

"Mom, you had her all to yourself last week when he was in the hospital. He hardly got to spend any time with her." I approached my mother slowly, putting my hand on her shoulder. "Don't be mad at him. He's not doing well."

"Don't touch me," she hissed, pulling away. "You're an unfit mother. I should take Lily away from you."

"You're not going to threaten me, Mom. Lily's my child, and you're never going to take her away from me." I gathered my things. She was still standing in the same place when I returned.

"You know, I didn't move to California just for the weather. I can't deal with your rage. It hurts me physically." I patted my stomach. "I've lived in constant fear of your mood swings. You've refused to get help, so you left me no choice but to get away from you. I think it would be best if we didn't talk for a while."

I stood there, waiting for her to respond, wanting something—a word, a hug, something. But she didn't move. I slammed my fist onto the counter.

"Why can't you just be happy like you were last night? Why do you always want to push me away?"

She kept staring at the coffee pot. There was no sign of reconciliation, and I turned to leave, damp from sweat. When I reached the door, her voice echoed through the narrow hallway.

"Go to hell."

* * *

## 1993

"May I speak to Sheryl Benson?" The female voice had a New York accent.

"This is she." I set down the stack of bills I was paying and closed the bedroom door.

"My name is Barbara Stratford. I'm a friend of your mother's."

"Did she ask you to call me?"

"Well, no . . . not really, but I think you might want to see her. She's not well, and she's all by herself, with the exception of me. I'm the only one who comes by anymore."

"That's what happens when you push people away," I said coolly.

"I know she can be a difficult person, but she is your mother."

"Barbara, I know you want to help, but you can't possibly understand the situation between my mother and me. Let me ask you a question. Is she still in a rage?"

The silence on the other end lingered. "Barbara?" I asked again.

"She's not a well woman. I don't think she can help herself."

I knew where this was going. It had happened before.

Every few years for the past decade I got a call from one of my mother's few friends trying to persuade me to call her. I felt sorry for Barbara.

"Barbara, I love my mother. I don't wish her bad, but this isn't something I can fix. I've sent her letters over the years to try to stay in touch with her, but she never responded. She stopped all contact with her granddaughter, too, who also sent her cards over the years."

"She doesn't have long. Don't you want to see her before she passes?"

"If she really wants to see me, all she has to do is call me and say that she loves me, and I'll be on the next flight."

"I understand. I don't know what's going to happen to your mother, but I don't blame you for how you feel. Thank you for letting me talk to you." Barbara hung up, and I went into the bathroom to blot my eyes with a tissue.

When I walked into the kitchen, Lily was sitting on the counter reading a magazine. College-bound and eager to leave home, she had often talked about going back east for her undergraduate studies. Though I kept my feelings to myself, the thought of her going so far away made me feel desperate to find a way to keep her here.

"Do you remember your grandmother Ava?" I asked.

Her face, so reminiscent of Ava's, looked at me with curiosity. "A little. She liked to play Sammy Davis or some kind of music like that. Isn't she the one who always said, 'Fifty million Frenchmen can't be wrong'?"

I could feel the tension dissipating in my body. The weight of guilt was just a little less. "You're right. She sure did. Your grandmother is quite a character."

"Do you miss her?"

I nodded. "Very much. I just can't argue and fight."

Lily wrapped her arms around me, like she used to when she was little. Though now she was quite a bit taller than me.

"As long as I have you—that's all I need," I said, holding onto her tightly.

Some people don't feel like they have closure until they say goodbye. A part of me knew that I would never speak to my mother again after that fateful morning in 1979. I had to let her go. It has gotten easier over the years, but I always left a little room for hope in case those fifty million Frenchmen tell me my mother has changed.

# THE PREACHER

It happened that he came to my office on a Thursday afternoon. Rhonda, who worked the front desk of the office building I rented, sounded unsettled when she phoned me about a man who wanted to see me.

"Send him in. I have some time before my next appointment," I said.

He walked with long, sweeping strides into my small office. He wore a white cotton T-shirt and blue jeans with a pair of heavy, black leather boots. An intricate design of an eagle was tattooed on his right upper arm. The smell of aftershave mixed with cigarettes wafted toward me. When he sat down, I could tell that he was evaluating the dingy, windowless room. I could hardly stand the place myself, with its peach-colored walls and musty odor, but the rent was what I could afford at the time.

"What can I do for you?" I asked.

He was looking at a framed picture of my wife Janice for a moment. When his attention shifted back to me, I moved uneasily in my seat. He was not a young man, but his body was thick with defined muscles, his graying brown hair slicked back. He had a square face with a pair of narrow, steely gray eyes and a thick beard that covered most of the bottom half of his face.

"My daughter was killed on Tuesday trying to catch the bus. The driver didn't stop, but someone got his license plate number and description of the car." He slid a wrinkled sheet of yellow paper across my cluttered desk. "I won't rest until something's been done."

"I'm so sorry. . ."

"Preach."

"Preach, this will certainly help," I said, reading the scrawled handwriting quickly. "How old was she?"

"Seven. Her name was Samantha."

As Preach relayed the details of the accident, I made some notes on my legal pad.

"I'm really sorry to hear about your daughter. I will do whatever I can, and I will get back to you in a day or so," I said.

When he stood up to leave, he shook my hand. His grip was tight, a little too tight. His forearm was noticeably bigger than mine. Yet, when I looked at his face, all I could see was a vulnerable man who had just lost his daughter.

"She was a smart girl. Much smarter than her old man."


My law practice was still new and the workload was light, as I had not yet had time to advertise or network. Yet Preach's case kept me busy. The man who killed his daughter was thirty-six-year-old Gary Suston, who had received a DUI less than five years ago. Since we were unable to settle out of court, the case went to trial. On the day of the trial, Preach arrived at the courthouse driving a shiny, black Harley Davidson, its engine roaring. He was wearing attire similar to what he wore when he came to my office. Throughout the entire process, Preach was cooperative, but also quiet, never saying more than what was necessary. I glanced at him a few times during the trial. His hands remained folded in front of him, his gaze fixed sometimes on the judge and sometimes on the defendant. When the verdict was announced, he looked at me, his eyes widening slightly. The heavy lines around his eyes and mouth stood out to me. They reminded me of cracks that would continue to multiply until his face shattered into dust.

"Thank you for everything you've done. I couldn't have asked for a better lawyer," Preach said. He shook my hand again.

"I'm glad the outcome was in your favor." I sounded rigid, uncertain. I patted his shoulder. I knew this moment would just be a respite from the pain he would have to endure for the rest of his life. I was a competent and generally successful lawyer, but I always had a vague sense that, despite my success, I was just merely playing my role in the legal system, cleaning up messes as best as possible. There was nothing I could do to make Preach feel whole again, and that realization always had a sobering effect on any victory I had as a lawyer.

A few weeks after the trial, Preach gave me a call asking if I would join him for a beer at his home. I never had contact with my clients after a trial, but I liked Preach. He was authentic. There were no pretenses when I spoke to him.

"Is he part of Hells Angels?" Janice asked when she heard me accept the invitation.

"Of course not. He wouldn't invite me to his house if he were. He looks rough, but he's actually a nice guy."

"You better not get on one of those bikes, Alex," she said, getting dressed to go to work at the public library.

"I won't, sweetheart," I said to her. "I know better than that."

When I drove up to his modest home, motorcycles similar

to his were parked in front. I carefully parked my twelve-year-old, rusty, brown Lincoln Continental between the sleek bikes. I felt like I had just docked the Queen Mary.

As I was admiring one of the motorcycles, another Harley with a matte black paint job, Preach opened the front door. He was carrying a beer in one hand and holding a cigarette in the other.

"Welcome," he said. "Have you ever been on a motorcycle?"

"No. I'm more of a Corvette person myself. My first car was a '59 Stingray." I saw him glance at my beat-up car, and I cringed a little. The faded paint spots were even more conspicuous under the late afternoon sun. I felt like I had to say something to distract him. "My wife and I just moved back to Phoenix from Los Angeles."

"Ah. . . L.A. is much different than Phoenix."

"Janice is a screenwriter, and I wanted to help her produce her films. So we moved there for a while to be in the right scene and network. We would sneak onto these movie studio lots. Sometimes we got lucky and had the opportunity to speak to some people."

Preach slapped my back hard enough that I swayed. When he laughed, it was with full force. His narrow eyes seemed to disappear in the web of wrinkles that lengthened as his cheeks and forehead lifted. His laugh was deep, and I could imagine the sound coming out of his mouth in even waves.

"Did you meet anyone famous?" he asked.

"Once we bumped into Steven Spielberg, but it was just for a few minutes. He's a nice guy."

I followed him into the house. One of the walls leading toward the kitchen was covered with photos of young Samantha and a woman who I assumed to be her mother. I hadn't realized until now that I still didn't know that much about Preach, whether he was still married or what his occupation was. A slender man wearing all black clothing leaned against the cupboard watching me. He extended his hand when Preach introduced us.

"They call me Flat Black, and that's Pollock over there smoking the cigar."

Pollock got up from his seat to shake my hand. My gaze immediately shifted to the silver chain dangling from his waist band, which was connected to a holster.

"I'm assuming that motorcycle with the matte paint job is yours." I turned to face Flat Black, so I wouldn't have to look at the gun.

"Sure is."

"So you're here to join Hells Angels?" Pollock asked in a thick Polish accent.

The beer paused in front of my mouth. "Huh?"

"It's no big deal. We just have a simple test, like initiation."

"But I can't even ride–"

"Christ, Pollock. He's an attorney. Don't mess with him," Preach said. "We're just a group of old men who like to get together and ride our bikes. We're our own group."

"What's with the gun?" I asked Pollock.

"For protection."

Flat Black rolled his eyes, "Yeah, for that stray coyote that wants to nibble on his leg. Pollock still thinks this is the Wild West."

Though I never felt quite part of the group, I at least started to relax around them, joining them for a game of pool in Preach's newly built Arizona room. Between beers, I learned a little about all of them. Flat Black and Pollock were in the landscaping business, and Preach operated heavy machinery, such as forklifts, on construction sites. People started calling him Preach because he was a wedding minister on the side. He also conducted funerals for his group.

I shared my own story: working for a large firm sixty hours a week and giving it all up because I believed in Janice and thought I could help her build her career. Now, I was returning to what I thought I knew best.

"Law is definitely not a profession for the timid," Preach said. "You gotta be a fighter."

"You definitely have to like confrontation," I replied, snapping the stick so that the striped ball bounced against the rail and rolled into one of the pockets.

"But you're good, Alex," Preach continued. "You have a presence about you. I saw the way people looked at you at the courthouse. You care."

I laughed a little, imagining Janice's surprised face to hear someone say that about me. She was so used to the quiet version of me. Toward the end of the night, Preach encouraged me to try out his motorcycle. The other two immediately joined in.

"Just around the block. No big deal," Preach insisted, as we followed him into the garage.

The bike was parked next to a beat-up orange Chevy pickup truck. The pristine black paint shined beneath the single bulb hanging from the ceiling. I sat down on the leather seat, listening to Preach talk about the mechanics of the bike. I could feel my body break out in a cold sweat as soon as I raised the kick stand, balancing the bike with my arms and legs.

"Just take your time," Preach said.

They all started whooping and clapping, as I rolled down the driveway onto the street. I didn't try going too fast, but the full exposure to the elements was still thrilling. The cool night air blew gently against my face and torso. The sweat immediately evaporated, leaving a trail of goose bumps on my arms. I rode up and down the *cul-de-sac* a couple of times before I let it coast back into Preach's driveway.

"Well, what do you think?" Pollock asked.

"It's great. But I'm a long way away from riding with you guys," I answered, swinging my leg off the bike.

"Give it some time. You'll be addicted to riding in no time," Flat Black joined in.

"We'll see," I said.

Although I didn't ride with the group after that visit, I spent time with them regularly, usually playing pool at Preach's house. Preach treated all his friends equally, as though the group were one family. Even though I felt that I was different from these people, I enjoyed being around them, especially Preach. Despite the loss of his daughter, he continued to live his life as best as he could. He wore a smile and laughed when we laughed, but sometimes I could see his eyes looking out in the distance, lost in thought. I felt so badly for him that I always looked away, too afraid to say anything.

"Midlife crisis, Mr. Levins?" Rhonda asked me one morning, as I grabbed my mail.

"Excuse me?"

"You're letting your hair grow. That's one of the signs."

I instinctively ran my hand over my hair, which now reached the top of my shoulders. The makeup she plastered on her face crinkled when she smiled.

*Well, I guess you might know, since you've already experienced yours*, I thought to myself. Instead of actually responding, however, I glared at her until she looked way. I hastily went to my office and shut the door. I really thought I did look better with longer hair.

The following week, I took Preach's motorcycle to a strip mall near his house, which had a large parking lot. Preach was kind enough to allow me to take the motorcycle when he didn't need to use it. I was beginning to really like riding a motorcycle, though I kept this fact from Janice. This time I allowed myself to go a little faster, swerving between the parking strips. My mind started drifting, imagining what I would tell Janice if I actually bought a motorcycle. She might try to throw something at me, like the coffee pot. Maybe she would like it if she had a chance—

A car was passing in front of me. My mind blanked, and I couldn't remember how to brake. I steered sharply to the right, just missing the back bumper of the car. A parking strip loomed just in front of me, and, before I could slow the bike, the front tire collided with the cement, pitching me over the handlebars. My right side smashed onto the asphalt. The adrenaline kicked in and, at first, I couldn't feel any pain. I rushed over to the bike, lying on its side. Some of the paint was chipped and scratched in a few places, but fortunately, there was no real damage. Something warm ran down the side of my face, and, when I pulled my hand away, it was covered in blood. I checked the rest of my wounds, and was relieved that nothing was broken. I was grateful that no one came to check on me. It was bad enough that Janice was going to have a field day with me.

I managed to drive the bike back to Preach and apologize profusely for the accident. If he was annoyed, he didn't show it to me. He checked my head wound and had me sit with him for a while before letting me go home.

"I'm really sorry, Preach. I'll pay for any damages," I said, getting into my car.

"I'm not worried about it. You didn't do that much damage. It could've been worse."

When I got home, I cleaned myself off as much as I could before Janice returned. I grabbed a beer and gently settled into my chair, closing my eyes.

"What happened to your face?" Janice was leaning over me, her face within inches of mine.

"Nothing. I fell."

"Uh-huh." She sat down across from me, folding her hands on her lap and glaring at me. "You got on that bike, didn't you? You need to see a doctor."

"It's just some bruising. Let it go. I'm tired, it's been a long day, and I really don't want to hear about it."

I kept shifting my legs, trying to find a position that wouldn't hurt my lower back. She crossed her arms over her chest, staring at me with that sharp expression that usually unsettles me. "I'm fine. I'm just hurting."

"I went to Dr. Lombard today. I'm pregnant, Alex."

I moved too quickly, a searing pain going down my right side. There were a myriad of things I felt, but all I could say was, "What do you want to do?"

She wiped the bottom of her eyes with her fingers, her lip tightening into a thin red line. "Why are you crying?" I said softly.

"Because you're not happy. This should be a happy occasion, and you look like I've just told you the worst news of your life!"

I moved next to her, wrapping my good arm around her. "I just never thought I would be in such a mess when this happened. I can hardly pay the bills and the—"

"Stop it! Our parents were worse off than we are, and they did just fine. You're afraid."

"Yes. All right. I'm afraid. I failed us, Janice. I took a big risk because I thought I was smart enough to help you find the right agent and the right people. I figured with enough work and time, we'd figure it out. But I failed—"

"*We* took the risk, Alex. We both made sacrifices."

"I'm trying to get our life together." The volume of my voice was climbing. "I'm starting a new practice. I can barely take care of us, let alone a child." I looked at our cramped living room in our small apartment, cluttered with furniture, newspapers and books, and rolled up movie posters. We had given up so much to pursue this dream; our house, our jobs, and most of our savings. We were starting all over. I shot up from the couch, pacing. Before I could even stop myself, I punched my fist through the closet door. The cheap wood gave in easily, and I managed to take out a sizeable chunk. I leaned my forehead against the door.

"I'm sorry, Janice."

"I'll always be grateful that you believed in me enough to do what you did. I'm still working at what I want to do, and we didn't fail. We're just following our dream in a different way."

Covering her mouth, she scurried down the hall. The bathroom door shut, and she started puking.

A few days later, I drove to Preach's house to give him a check for the damages on the bike. His brows furrowed, when I handed him the envelope.

"You don't owe me anything, Alex. It's just a scratch. I'm relieved you weren't badly hurt," he said, trying to return the check to me.

"No, I insist. I really feel bad. I guess I'm not meant to ride motorcycles."

He shrugged, but he was still looking at me closely. "What's going on? You look like something is bothering you."

He sat down on one of the lawn chairs on the porch, slipping a cigarette in his mouth. It was the first time I noticed he had a slight tremor in his hands. He nodded toward the empty chair beside him, and I sat down.

"Janice is pregnant, and I'm just not ready to start . . ." I realized what I was saying and immediately started apologizing.

"I lost my child, but that doesn't mean other people can't have children. I'm happy for you, Alex. You deserve to have your own family."

"How—How do you cope?"

"I drink, I work, and I ride that bike. Is that coping? I don't know." He leaned forward in his chair, smoking. "But you know what? I'll never regret having her in my life. When she was little, really little, she used to talk gibberish. Maybe she heard some Spanish and was trying to imitate it. But she would talk like this for *hours*. I would hear her in the bedroom having this 'conversation.' I never had a clue what she was talking about, but she sure seemed excited."

"Sounds like she had quite the imagination."

"Oh, she did. Must have gotten that from her mom." He seemed to be looking off in the distance, his mind already far away.

Though I never smoked much in my life, I pulled one out from Preach's pack and we sat there quietly. I was content just sitting with him.

"You were the second lawyer I saw that day," he said. "The first one didn't even say that he was sorry about what happened. He just looked at his calendar and said that he would see if he could take my case. But you cared, and you helped me during a difficult time. You're a good man, Alex. Give yourself some credit."

His tanned, hardened face softened, his mouth smiling weakly.

"Thank you," I said, bowing my head. "Sometimes I realize how much of my life has passed. How much I have left. The future Janice and I used to talk about when we first got married is already here. I feel like I've run out of time, and I have to wonder if I did right by the choices I made."

"There is no 'right.' You have a lot, Alex. Enjoy it. Enjoy everything you can. That's the only advice I can give you."

On my way home, I thought about what I would say to Janice. When I got inside the house, she was sitting at the kitchen table paying bills. I still couldn't think of the words I wanted to say, but she started to smile. We both realized that something in me had changed, if even slightly. The weight of my frustration and the desperate grip of my failures lifted.

Preach was truly a preacher. He lived, loved, and lost, and yet he still had so much to give. His gift to me was an eagerness to look forward, have some faith, and just trust the human existence.

# A PLACE OF THEIR OWN

*House*

Every Sunday after lunch, I laid down in the backseat of my parents' car as they drove through the nicer neighborhoods looking at the houses, which were much bigger than our small home. They dreamed about finding a house, a place that they could make their own.

"Can you imagine having a big enough space where we can finally put up those shelves?" My mother said wistfully.

My father looked at me through the rear-view mirror, "You know, when we finally move into a bigger house, I'll let you paint your room any color you want."

"Really? No more white walls?" I sat up in my seat. I hated white walls. I always had to keep them white in case they decided to put our house on the market. I immediately started fantasizing about painting my future room a shade of mint green and sticking glow-in-the-dark stars on the ceiling. "When do we get to move?"

"As soon as we find something we like and can afford," my

father answered. "It might take some time, but I won't give up. Never give up on anything that's really important to you."

When my parents finally bought their dream house, I was in college, but every summer and during the holidays I came back home and lived with them. The house was everything that my parents always wanted. It was much bigger than what we were used to. But it was also a "fixer upper." The project did not deter my parents. Every evening after work, my father sat at the kitchen table or in front of his computer with his yellow legal pad and black ball point pen. We often sat together, and, while I did my homework for school, he created his master plan for the renovation of our new home.

"It's going to be perfect. We'll be in that house in five months," he promised, his voice resounding with triumph and his eyes beaming with excitement for the future.

### The Moon and the Stars

Eleven months later, the renovation was still not done, but the house was at least livable. Up until the move, I had not been able to see my room. Everyone was still occupied unloading the truck and moving the boxes into the house. I slowly walked down the hallway, dragging the suitcase of things that were too precious to go into the moving truck.

I pushed the door open several inches and peered in. A black light lamp was attached to the wall and a shade of violet flooded half the ceiling, which was dotted with glow-in-the-dark paint to make it look like a constellation. I walked around the room, keeping my head tilted toward the ceiling. It looked far better than I could have ever imagined. I never wanted to leave this room.

I lay down on my bed, put my arms behind my head, and

gazed at the stars. It was a beautiful room, even if I only got to enjoy it for seven days.


## The Flood

The smell was like a shadow, following me everywhere I went inside that house. The odor had started gradually, but it smelled most strongly in my room. I sniffed my armpits and looked around me to find an answer to this mystery. The odor was pungent, a mixture of sweet and bitter. Sometimes it made me nauseous or dizzy. During those moments, I ran outside and lay down on the cool lawn, inhaling the fragrance of grass through my nostrils. But no matter how bad the odor was, I was determined not to surrender that room. All of my belongings were finally in their right place. I thought I could learn to live with the persistent stench. It was impossible.

My father and I stood in my bedroom one night, where the odor was most intense. We looked in every direction. We were on the hunt.

"It's coming from over there. I'm sure of it." I pointed at the air vent above us.

He crossed his arms over his chest and shook his head sadly.

A few days later, an air duct specialist climbed into the attic, a space crowded with fiberglass insulation, air ducts, electrical wires, and wooden planks. We heard his footsteps from above for several minutes. When he climbed down, he ran directly to one of the bathrooms. I covered my mouth when I heard the sound of puking. He finally came out of the room, wiping his flushed cheeks with a handkerchief.

"There's piss everywhere in your attic. There are stains on the structure of the house. But I also found puddles, which have already begun to turn into sludge. It's like the workers had a pissing contest up there, over and over again. I've never seen anything like it in my entire life."

## Proof

I tiptoed down the hallway toward the kitchen where my parents met with their insurance adjuster and a remediation specialist.

"I'm sorry to hear about your trouble, but I just can't believe that anyone would do such a thing, especially since you're suggesting that more than one person did this. Perhaps you have a rodent infestation." The insurance adjuster folded his arms over his bulging belly.

My mother shot a glance at the specialist, "Okay then, bring me the head of one turd. Prove to me that we have a rodent issue."

Not one specialist ever found the head of one turd. In fact, no one ever found any evidence of rodents, just urine. Human urine.

## Shattered Glass

My mother moved me to the spare room, which was still crowded with unpacked boxes. The smell was less intense here on the other side of the house, but the dust from the boxes made me sneeze. I brought what I could from my bedroom, but most of the belongings had to stay behind.

"You're not to go back in that room," she warned.

"I feel like I'm in exile," I muttered as she turned to leave. I knew it was just a room, a space with four walls. Yet, I had made it my own. A part of me was still left in that room. I looked down the hallway at the closed door to my room. I hoped that they wouldn't have to tear down the ceiling with my beautiful stars.

A team of workers in protective hazmat suits hauling heavy machinery arrived to remediate the house. Twenty negative air machines were set up to pull out the foul air. They started in the area of my bedroom, where the sludge was heavier. The room was sealed off from the rest of the house with sheets of plastic and yellow tape. It was a crime scene now. None of us could go in there, except the workers. Loud, distracting machine noises emanated from the room continuously from early morning until nighttime while they tore out the drywall first. After they stripped the room, the workers moved into the attic. All of the insulation had to be removed, and the stained wood had to be replaced or sealed with a biocide. At the end of each week, my father went into the room to see if the odor was diminishing. But every week came the same report: it still smelled.

I grew accustomed to the sound of their footsteps above. They were part of the house. Occasionally, the weight of their steps created vibrations that wreaked havoc below.

"Watch out!" I pushed my mother away from the counter just as a ceiling light crashed onto the floor. I felt as though the house were coming alive, venting its frustration by throwing parts of itself at us.

We shielded our heads with our hands and looked up to see if anything else was going to fall.

"I can't take this anymore," my mother muttered, sweeping the shards of glass into the trash. "It's been three months, and it still reeks of urine, despite all the remediation."

Now the odor was throughout the house, moving from area to area. One day a room would be safe, and then the next day the foul odor would permeate the space and chase us out of the room.

## *Affliction*

The house was rejecting us. Rashes developed on our arms. They looked like infected scabs. They itched, and sometimes I scratched them until they bled. Even though it was summer, we all started wearing long sleeves to avoid having to explain our complicated situation. Who would believe us, anyway? Whoever heard of a family losing their house to urine?

## *Bare Bones*

After five months, the remediator suggested that we move out of the house for a while so that they could tear down more of the walls, maybe all of them. No matter how bad the smell was, no one wanted to move. We loved that home. We had dreams.

On my way to bed one night, I saw light coming through the crack under the door. I carefully separated the plastic and opened the door. The room had been stripped down to blocks and wooden planks. The ceiling and walls were gone, as were my stars. I wondered what happened to all of my belongings, my bed, books, and other things that I couldn't take with me.

There was still the old pungent stench of urine, but now I could detect other odors. Besides the fresh wood, I could smell the biocide.

I started to feel like I wasn't alone, and when I turned around, I saw my father sitting on a crate. His hands covered his face.

"Are we going to lose the house?" I asked.

"I'm trying everything not to let that happen. I just don't know what to do next."

"What about my books? My stuff?"

"They had to remove them for testing, to make sure they aren't contaminated. Hopefully you'll get them back."

I folded my arms over my chest, but he didn't seem to notice the hostile expression on my face. He remained silent, looking off into the distance. We sat there together looking out the window for several minutes. He got up slowly and put his hand on my shoulder.

"It's going to be okay. At least we have our health."

"For the moment," I responded and I left him alone in the room.


*Sleep Monster*


By the sixth month the odor in my parents' room increased so that they had to find somewhere else to sleep. My mother moved the bed into another room. We were all exhausted from the stress. My mother broke up the day with naps. I pushed myself to stay awake so that perhaps the exhaustion would help me get through the night. Yet every night, I expressed my frustration through sleepwalking. Sometimes I even broke into a run. During one of these episodes, I ran into the end table in the living room, making a nose dive for the carpet. When I came to, my knee cap had swollen to the size of a softball. I didn't bother to wake anyone. I grabbed ice from the freezer and hobbled to the sofa. The pain was too much. The couch was too narrow and hard. I stayed up the rest of the night, watching the sun rise through the window.

*Dibs*

Apparently, none of us had slept well the night before. By the afternoon, the three of us were zombies, walking aimlessly through the house. My mother went into her room, asking that we give her space so she could decompress.

"I think I'm going to take a nap," my father said. I was wrapping my knee in bandages and ice.

"Where?"

"The spare room," he replied.

"But I wanted to take a nap. I didn't sleep last night."

"Neither did I. Your old man is really tired. Can't you take a nap later?"

I stood up, putting all my weight on my good leg, "Dibs! I called it." I started to hobble toward the room. I could hear his footsteps chasing me. We landed on the bed at the same time. Hysterical laughter, mixed with crying, filled the room.

"This is pitiful," he admitted.

"You don't say."

We continued laughing until consciousness slipped away from us. My mother woke us up later. She was leaning on the door frame, chewing her lower lip.

"You know, we're going to be reduced to sleeping in the closet if this keeps up," she said.

"I'm sorry," my father said. I wasn't sure exactly what he was apologizing for.

My father slowly sat up, rubbing his low back. He moved like an old man these days. I pressed the pillow on top of my face.

"Are you getting up? I'm making dinner," my mother said to me.

"Can you turn off the lights?" I mumbled through the pillow.

Though I couldn't see her, I could hear her sadness in the way she shuffled out of the darkened room. I could escape this mess. I was young and starting my own life. But what about them? This was their life. There wasn't anything I could do.

The house was not a dream house, but I learned that not all dreams lead to happiness. I hoped my parents would find other dreams. Another home. They were still young, I prayed.

# WANDERLUST

Arpeggio / Arsis / Aspiring

"Arsis is the unaccented part of a metrical foot," the guitarist, Landon, explained to me.

Landon practiced his arpeggios on a beat-up, black-and-white Epiphone before every show. It was part of his performance ritual.

"That's the first time I've ever heard of that musical term," I said, raising my voice over the relentless sound of Landon's metronome.

After a few more minutes of listening to the constant beeping, I grabbed the metronome to turn it off. Landon immediately looked up with a shocked expression.

"Calm down. Just give me a couple of minutes," I said, turning on the recording function on my phone. "So, how does it feel to be on your first nationwide tour?"

Landon rested his guitar across his lap. "I like being on the road, but this will be the longest I've ever been away from home. I hope this tour helps us out. We really need it." He gulped his energy drink and then burped loudly. "I've always wanted to go on a European tour. They absolutely love heavy metal over there. I'm sure we'd get a lot of fans if we went on a European tour."

We were nowhere near Europe. We were in the green room in a bar called Jack's Shack in Jacksonville, Florida. Landon picked up the guitar again and looked at me as he switched on the metronome. Since the couch was missing a cushion, I perched myself on the arm and watched Landon's nimble fingers dance over the strings.

## Band / Bass / Brother

"The first thing you should know is that the bass is just a dumb man's guitar," Landon said to me in front of Ellison, the bass player, as they stuffed their gear into a trailer.

I pulled out my notebook and started taking notes. I was an aspiring writer, and I had convinced the band to let me travel with them so I could document their first real touring experience.

"The other thing you should know is that the fastest way to shut Landon up is to put sheet music in front of him. None of these guys know how to read music except me." The bass player beamed proudly. "I was classically trained, and I can play the upright bass as well as the piano."

"You're such a snob," Landon retorted.

No one in the band really showed any serious animosity toward each other. They behaved like brothers. They had known each other since the fourth grade. However, sometimes the teasing got too much. Tempers flared, especially when they were short on money and couldn't afford food until the next gig. Just yesterday the singer, Birdie, punched the drummer because he had spent the gas money on a round of tequila shots. The drummer had sprawled out on the asphalt and laughed carelessly.

"Ah, man. We have enough until tomorrow."

They made up shortly afterward. The drummer bought the singer a beer at the next stop and they acted as though nothing happened.

They really loved each other.

## Chords / Cluster / Crazy

Dallas, the drummer, was the youngest member in the band. He had just turned twenty-five. A cluster of tattoos covered most of his scrawny figure. He claimed that they reminded him that he had to succeed in music because he couldn't fit in anywhere else. He lost most of his hearing in his left ear, but he still refused to wear earplugs because they made him feel disoriented.

"I used to sneak into scrap yards and run around hitting everything. Man, beating stuff up is the best feeling in the world." He stretched his body across the bed in a motel in Baton Rouge as I interviewed him.

"Is that why you chose the drums?" I asked.

"Birdie needed a drummer, so I gave it a try. It came easily to me. It's the only thing in my life that ever came easily to me." He yawned and closed his eyes. He looked like he could fall asleep in seconds.

I tapped his foot with my pen to keep him awake. "Hey! One more question. Did you ever wish you picked a different instrument?"

"No way!" The question seemed to rouse him awake. He sat up on his elbow. "I was meant to be a drummer just like Landon was meant to play guitar. We all have roles to play.

That's the way I see it."

As I put away my notebook and recorder, I caught a whiff of his body odor, a bizarre combination of sweat, alcohol, and hand sanitizer.

"You finally have access to a shower. You might want to take advantage of it," I suggested.

He sniffed his armpit and shrugged. Then, squinting at me, "You hitting on me?"

"I can smell all of you from ten feet away. I don't think you'll ever get the B.O. out of that RV."

Though the smell was strong, I was too exhausted to care and collapsed on the far side of the bed. He rolled onto his side, sliding his hand toward me.

"No," I said again. "I'm a writer. I'm here to document your cross-country tour. That's it."

"What do you think about all of this?" When he smiled, it was the first time I noticed he was missing one of his back teeth.

"It's exhausting. I don't know how you keep going."

Dallas moved his shoulders up in a slight shrug, "I don't think it's so bad. I wouldn't mind doing this for the rest of my life. I just want to play music."


Dashboard / Deep Purple / Dumb


The headlights stopped working. Every night while one of them was driving, I crouched in the front seat near a mass of exposed wires under the dashboard. When a car was approaching, the driver gave me the warning, and I had to connect two of the wires to turn on the headlights.

Today it was the singer's turn to drive. Everyone called him Birdie, but his real name was Bart.

"So, what are you guys going to do when this tour is over?" I asked.

"Go back home. I'll take my old job back for a while. There's this small shop that sells Asian imports. The pay's bad, but the couple who owns it are real cool about me coming and going. They always take me back." He swallowed the rest of his Monster Java. Some of it dribbled down his chin, now spotted with stubble. He played with the radio dial until he found a station. The familiar chords from Deep Purple's "Smoke on the Water" wavered over the tinny speakers.

"This is the first song I learned to play on the guitar." Birdie smiled blissfully as he wiped his chin with his sleeve. "Actually, it's the only song I can play."

### Ellison / Evade / Expression

Ellison Roberts, the bass player, was addicted to Butterfingers and roasted almonds. He didn't like to talk much, but he'd share his almonds with me. He would absolutely never share his Butterfingers. No one was allowed to even touch those.

I don't know much about the bass, but when I watched Ellison pluck and tap the thick steel strings during the concerts, I thought he played just as hard as Landon. Bass players don't get enough credit. It's always the singer and guitarist that the crowd rushes after a show.

### Fear / Finger / Frets

Blood dribbled down the fret board of the guitar. One of the calluses on Landon's finger cracked, spilling fat droplets of blood. My own fingertips began to hurt as I watched him play. He didn't seem to care, or maybe he hadn't noticed it yet.

Suddenly, he stopped playing and looked at me as though he had forgotten that I had been watching him.

"Hey, how come you aren't in a band? Don't you play the sax or something?" He asked.

"The piano," I corrected him. "It's a little hard to tour with a piano."

"Totally, man," he said lazily. "That's why keyboards are so much cooler. They're even easier to move than an entire guitar rig."

"I could never do what you do. I have terrible performance anxiety." I bit my lower lip. Just thinking about being on stage made my mouth go dry.

"And you think we don't get nervous? Why do you think we all act so weird before a show? We're all nervous," Landon said. It was the first time I saw him really smile.

"How do you do it?" I asked.

Landon put his guitar back in the case. "You learn to use the anxious energy to your advantage. You don't want to reach the point where you stop feeling the butterflies in your stomach. That's when it's over."

### Gig / Gold / Guitar

In addition to his Epiphone guitar, Landon owned a Gold Starburst Gibson that he wouldn't let anyone play or even touch. It was his prized possession. When he took it out of its case, I tried not to stare at it. He only used the guitar for "important" gigs, though I never figured out what he defined as an important show.

When I was twelve, I bought an acoustic Washburn guitar at a garage sale. I had become obsessed with Grace Slick and Joan Jett. My mother never said a word about the guitar, but a month later it went missing. I have no proof, but I'm sure my mother got rid of it when she heard me trading my piano practices for guitar lessons with the next-door neighbor who impersonated Jerry Garcia for a living. My mother argued rock and roll wasn't real music.

## Happy / Head / Houston

All of our heads are pounding, but we're still feeling the residual happiness from last night. It was the first time on the tour that the band played for a packed venue. Birdie pulled over six times so one of us could throw up on the side of the road. I can't remember all that we drank last night after the gig in Houston, but I do recall several six packs of Blue Ribbon beer. At least I remember a ribbon on the front of the can, but maybe it wasn't blue . . .

## Imperfect / Interlude / Instruments

"Music is imperfect because humans are imperfect," Ellison argued while admiring the instruments in a pawnshop. He repeatedly went back to an upright bass leaning against the wall.

Landon knelt on the floor to examine a cherry red Kramer guitar. "That's stupid, man. Shredding is about precision and perfection. That's why I practice for hours every day. I think you can create the perfect song. They're called radio hits."

"I think both of you are right," I interjected as I watched Ellison plucking one of the strings on the bass. "Music doesn't have to be perfect. It just has to make you feel something. When I think about some of my favorite songs, they feel like a beautiful escape from life. Maybe there's something about how music affects us that feels like perfection."

"You can learn a lot about a person by the music they listen to and how they play," Ellison added.

That night at a friend's house, they practiced new material for their next show. Landon added an interlude, which was more like a solo that continued for several minutes. The others slowed their playing and then gradually stopped. But Landon didn't know when to stop, and he kept playing even after the others went outside to drink and smoke.

## Jenny / Journey / Jubilee

I told the band that my name was Jenny. My real name is Jubilee Winters. No one takes a Jubilee seriously. I don't even look like a Jubilee. I wear all black. Even my naturally blond hair is dyed black.

I like music, but I don't feel it the same way these guys do. They feel it so strongly that they can improvise anything anytime they want. I can't. I need sheet music. Structure. Rules. I'm more of a conformist than I want to believe.

## Key / Kingdom / KitKat

The gas station didn't have any Butterfingers or almonds, so Ellison bought KitKat bars instead. This time he tossed me a pack and we ate silently, leaning against the front bumper of the RV. The flat desert surrounded us. The sun was on top of us, heavy and unrelenting. I could already feel the population of freckles growing exponentially on my arms and face. As I sucked on the chocolate, I instinctually fingered my house keys in my pocket. I hadn't used my keys in weeks, but I still liked to keep them in my pocket. I missed home.

## Labor / Lines / Love

Everyone in the band had a different job. Birdie was in charge of marketing. In every city, he posted hundreds of flyers in music stores, colleges, bars, and parking lots. The flyers were postcard-sized and in black and white. Birdie's goal that summer was to sell over two thousand CDs.

"What about the cafes?" I suggested.

"We're a metal band. Metalheads don't hang out in cafes." He covered someone else's flyer with his own because there were no empty spaces left on the bulletin board. The lines on his forehead deepened.

"What?" I asked.

"Sometimes it hits me, and I think that maybe we're all crazy. Who thinks it's a great idea to quit their job and tour in an RV to become rock stars?"

"Musicians," I answered.

Birdie laughed. "Exactly. I love what I do, but I know I can't do it forever. I'm giving myself until I'm thirty."

"Why thirty?" I asked, sticking a flyer beneath a car windshield.

"At some point you have to grow up."

## Mane / Maple / Music

There's a "Friends don't let friends cut their hair" bumper sticker on the back of Landon's amplifier. He is the only one with hair past his shoulders. It's thick and the color of vanilla maple. During the shows he moves his head in a circle so that he looks like a windmill. You never see his face, even when he's standing still.

## Naked / Noise / Notes

Lately the shows have been more packed. The band is gaining momentum. But success doesn't always make them happy. Musicians are naked warriors, thinly veiled by the notes they play on their instruments.

Behind the venue, as people left to go home, Dallas asked me to hold his hand while the effects of whatever he took faded. His green Mohawk wilted from perspiration. Every time he heard a noise, he jumped or twitched. Even my whistling bothered him.

## Onion / Oompah / Opportunity

"It's like peeling an onion. There are layers," I explained to Ellison when he asked about my progress documenting their band. "Every day I get to know you guys a little better, a little closer to the core."

"But why write about us? We haven't made it. We may never make it." He took a long sip from his beer and held the glass to his forehead. Until recently he never drank before the show, but now he has at least two drinks before he gets onstage.

"That's the whole point. This is the most interesting phase of a band's journey. There's not enough room for every band to have a successful career, so you're all fighting for a piece of that limited space. I don't think people understand the extent to which you all make sacrifices just to have the opportunity to play."

Ellison shrugged and nodded. The members from the opening band started their sound check. A slender girl with curly black hair swayed to the rhythm of oompahs coming from her trombone. The sound was low and made me think of soft velvet.

"I think I'm in love," Ellison said, a little beer dribbling down his chin as his eyes remained transfixed on the trombone player.


Pages / Phoenix / Piano

I proudly thumbed through the pages of my spiral notebook, which was now filled with notes and observations of the band. I have always preferred writing by hand than on the computer. The physical act of pressing the pen against the paper to track my thoughts makes me feel more grounded in my writing.

We reached Phoenix today. There are few parks and pretty places. Most of the buildings are gray concrete cubes. The roads are super wide, and there are enormous parking lots everywhere, like Tarmac lakes.

At a small and nearly empty cafe, I ended my long separation with the piano. When I thought no one was looking, I sat down and felt the smooth keys with my fingertips. I played just one song. I couldn't remember anything else.

## Queen / Quirk / Quit

At their concert in Phoenix, Mistress Annihilation was the MC for the show. Her real name was Crystal, but in the heavy metal community she was known as Mistress Annihilation, the Queen of Metal. Every week she interviewed a band for her web show. She never played an instrument in her life, but she knew everything about rock music. She often wore corsets, thigh-high boots, and miniskirts made out of black patent leather. Her voice was low and raspy, and she punctuated every other sentence by making the sign of the horns with her long-manicured fingers and sticking out her tongue. Tonight, she introduced the bands for the show.

When the guys smoked outside, they talked about her, imitating her quirks. Birdie suddenly started coughing after his second cigarette.

"I really need to quit," he claimed, "just after I finish this pack."

## Realize / Road / Rock

I found a message in my notebook last night:

*I think you're pretty metal, for a girl, of course. I'm glad you're with us. You are kind of like our rock, even though you don't talk much. Why is that? Is that why you write? Because you're too afraid to say things out loud? Where will you go when you've reached the end of the road with us?*

As I examined the penmanship, I realized I had never seen the guys write anything except their autographs when they sold band merchandise. Under different circumstances, I'd be upset if someone went through my belongings, but over the course of the past several weeks we had seen each other at our worst and most vulnerable. It meant something to me that someone in the band saw me so clearly.

## Self / Seven / Shadow

Landon liked to tell me about his multiple identities, which he described as his army of shadows that followed him everywhere. When he was seven, therapists put him on different medications to make him less hyper. But the drugs just made him more rambunctious.

"You could say the shadows are like different voices that live inside my head. Sometimes one voice gets louder and takes control. Like when I'm onstage I'm one person, and when I'm offstage I'm another person. I think everyone is that way to some extent. Maybe they just don't know it," Landon said.

Landon and I sat at the tiny, square kitchen table inside the RV. The bathroom door swung open and Birdie stepped out, laughing and shaking his head at Landon.

"I've known this dude since we were ten years old. He's got only one personality and it's always about him." Birdie patted the back of Landon's shoulder and left the RV without waiting for Landon's response.

Landon crossed his arms over his chest and rolled his eyes. "They just don't get me sometimes. I think they're a little jealous of me."

"Hmm. . ." I pressed my lips together to suppress a laugh.

## Thigh / Trust / Tucson

Last night Ellison and I sat outside, since we were not in the mood to be inside a bar. The outside of our thighs touched. The air was still hot and dry, and the dust stuck to the back of our throats, making us thirsty. We stared at the strip mall across the street with its shops closed for the evening.

"Who chooses to live in Tucson?" Ellison asked.

"Apparently college students and people who don't want to live in Phoenix," I answered lazily.

"So, what do you do when you're not touring with a bunch of crazy dudes?" Ellison asked.

For a moment I had forgotten what I did before this tour. Home felt like a distant world. Being on the road had required all of my energy and attention.

"Data entry," I answered flatly.

Ellison's upper lip curled in sneer. "Sounds like a blast."

I shrugged my shoulders. "It's a job, but the health benefits are pretty good."

Ellison didn't respond. We sat in silence for a while until I started to feel antsy. I looked at his thin, muscular forearms wrapped in thick, blue veins. His right thumbnail was completely blue.

"It was you who wrote in my notebook," I said suddenly.

Ellison didn't turn to look at me, but I thought I could see the edge of his mouth subtly turn upward.


## Unsettled / Urge / Used

After our show in San Diego, we parked the RV for the night at a truck stop. It was three o'clock in the morning, and the guys were physically drained and immediately passed out.

I hadn't showered in four days, and the urge to wash my hair was so strong that I couldn't sleep. I quietly grabbed my things and stepped out of the RV. Rows of trucks purred loudly as their generators ran through the night. I walked past the semis, feeling both mesmerized and unsettled by the scene.

I half expected someone to accost me, but I didn't see another human except for the woman behind the register. She was still young, but the matronly dress she wore made her look older.

The showers at this particular truck stop were spacious and well sanitized. I stood beneath the shower head and let the strong pressurized water wash away the layer of grime. When I got back to the RV, Ellison lifted his head off the pillow and rubbed his eyes.

"Shh. . ." I whispered as I found a space on the couch to lay down. I was so tired now that I craved sleep more than anything else in the world at the moment.

"Are the showers any good?" Ellison asked.

"The best. . ." I mumbled, pulling the covers around myself like a cocoon shutting out the light.


Vanilla / Verona / Vigorous

Everyone practiced regularly, but Landon practiced several hours every day except when it was his turn to drive. His regimen was vigorous: two hours of scales (with a metronome) and alternate picking, two hours practicing the band's material, and another two hours writing new songs. Nothing got between him and his practices, except his girlfriend, Verona. They hadn't been together for very long. His cheeks always burned red when she phoned him.

"Things are going great. People really like us on the West Coast." I could hear him say to Verona. " . . . oh, but we're not moving or anything. I'm just saying they're much more open here. We'll be back in a couple weeks. I promise."

He was snarky when he caught me watching him.

"What?" I exclaimed. "It's cute. There's nothing wrong with being cute."


## Wanderlust / Want / Whistle

No one wants to go home. They are consumed by wanderlust and that euphoric feeling of playing in front of enthusiastic crowds. After their last show, they sat on the edge of the stage with their rigs stacked and packed in piles. A few people stayed until closing. One of them was an attractive blond who approached Landon coyly. He smiled shyly, and she sat on his lap, brushing her lacquered lips against his face.

While we packed the trailer for the last time, Landon disappeared. He returned a few hours later, his pale neck bruised and a little bit of that want still flashing in those pale gray eyes.


## Xerox / X-rated / X-ray

Nothing about home feels real anymore. On the kitchen table, my mother left a Xerox of her X-ray. A small, grayish blur was circled several times with a red felt tip pen.

"It almost looks phallic," my mother said, carrying a bag loaded with groceries.

"Is it cancer?"

"It's benign, but the doctor needs to remove it because it's putting pressure on my right lung. It should be a quick procedure. You can take care of the house while I recover." Her voice was calm.

I nodded automatically, running my finger over the image. I took a deep breath, but my lungs wouldn't take in the oxygen. I kept inhaling until my body released a yawn.

## Yawn / Yoke / Young

The "short" procedure lasted ten hours. While she was healing, my mother and I pretended that everything was all right. One day she said that she was worried about me. When I asked her why, she didn't answer immediately. I gave up after a while and dumped Ovaltine into my glass until the milk turned to mud.

"I just want you to be happy," she said.

"I am. I'm just a little stuck."

## Zephyr / Zero / Zombie

When you're not where you're supposed to be, you turn into a zombie. I function like a well-oiled machine, but inside I feel completely empty. Every evening I pull out the documentary, thumbing through the pages and rereading certain passages. The pressure to get it right weighs heavily on me. Somehow, I'm afraid to begin. I'm stuck at zero.

I think about what the band might be doing now. I imagine them touring the country in their RV, scraping by but always managing to make it work. It's a hard life, but a part of me misses it.

Now and again, I feel the urge to pick up and go. The moments are brief and subtle, like a zephyr in the unrelenting, predictable pattern of my life. I wish I knew what these urges really meant.

# REAL MAN

Outside of the restaurant, Dakota scrutinized her reflection in the window. She wished she hadn't chosen such a tight-fitting dress. She was not accustomed to holding in her stomach, but she really wanted to look her best for this date. She adjusted her face mask and checked her phone for the third time in five minutes. Dakota hated to be late, so she made sure that she would be at the restaurant a few minutes early. Except now, she felt that by arriving before her date, it made her appear desperate.

Dakota shoved her hand into her purse to reach for her phone a fourth time, when she noticed a man walking toward her. He was tall and wore a navy blue suit with a white button-down shirt.

Extending his hand toward Dakota the man said, "Hello, Dakota. My name is Brad. How are you doing this evening?"

Though half of his face was covered with a mask, his light brown eyes creased in a way to suggest that he was smiling. Dakota was surprised by the warmth of his hand. "It's nice to meet you. I hope you like sushi."

"Of course," he responded.

When they reached the entrance to the restaurant, Brad reached for the door to hold it open for her. He moved so gracefully that Dakota paused in admiration before stepping past the threshold.

As soon as they were seated, they removed their face masks. Dakota watched Brad neatly fold and then tuck the face covering into his jacket pocket. His face was attractive, but what caught Dakota's attention more was how warm his gaze felt when he looked at her.

A waitress stopped by to fill their glasses with water and take their order. Dakota nervously took a sip of her water.

"So, what do you do when you're not on a date?" Dakota asked.

"I'm training to work with other humanoids to help them better adapt to their new situations."

"I see," Dakota mused. "So, do you wear a face covering to blend in?"

"Yes. While I'm not susceptible to diseases, I prefer people to think I'm just like them," Brad answered.

"Wow! Artificial intelligence has come a very long way."

"We prefer to be called *transhuman*. Artificial intelligence suggests that we're not real or that we're merely just a copy of a human. It's true that machines made me, but humans were the ones to develop the technology," Brad explained patiently.

"Oh! I didn't know. I'm sorry if I offended you," Dakota responded sheepishly.

"Not at all. We're a recent addition to society. Of course, it will take time for people to get used to us. We're really more like humans than you would think. We just have a different origin."

Out of a nervous habit, she twisted the ring on her right

hand. She wasn't sure she believed that he could feel like a human. Where did the programming end and his own beliefs and emotions begin? Was there even a line between the two?

About two months ago, while sitting in the waiting room of her gynecologist's office, Dakota saw a dating ad in a fashion magazine. Real Man was a state-of-the-art tech company that created the perfect male humanoid for the busy professional woman who didn't want to settle for less than she deserved. Real Man offered a selection of attractive and cultured male humanoids to rent for dates and events. They also offered custom made-to-order male humanoids for women looking for permanent mates. After completing a payment plan, the company mailed the customer a marriage certificate.

Dakota's initial reaction was laughter. Her face mask billowed as a guffaw escaped her lips. How ridiculous, she thought. Who in their right mind would do such a thing? Dakota dropped the magazine on the coffee table and selected another magazine. She would rather adopt a bunch of cats and become the archetypal crazy cat lady than go on a date with a robot.

Two months later, Dakota had a change of heart. At the encouragement of her friends, she went out on a date with a guy she met on Plenty of Fish. He went by the name Mickey. They met for lunch at a trendy Italian restaurant. Halfway through the meal, Mickey said that he forgot his wallet, but that he would make up for it the next time. Dakota wasn't even sure that she wanted a next time, but she tried to give him the benefit of the doubt and remain open-minded. A week went by, however, and Dakota didn't hear anything from him. Instead, he randomly texted her a photo of his nether regions, traumatizing Dakota's sensibilities for the rest of the day.

Was this the new standard? Dakota thought about the

number of times her friends came to her with their marital and relationship woes. "So and so" is addicted to pornography and no longer wants to have sex with his wife, or "so and so" refuses to hold down a job, or "so and so" will never pick up after himself. Dakota wondered why she would even want to be in a relationship if she had to put up with such behavior. When she told her friends that she would never settle and that she would patiently wait for the right one to show up in her life, her friends laughed at her naivete and declared that all men are basically the same.

Dakota had a glass of wine before she called the number for Real Man.

"This is Elaine, your representative for Real Man. How can I help you?"

"I saw your ad in a magazine, and I had some questions," Dakota said. She felt the butterflies in her stomach and poured herself another glass of wine.

"Are you interested in a date, relationship, or marriage?" Elaine asked.

"A date! I'm not ready for that kind of commitment. I just want to try it out." As she heard the words came out of her mouth, Dakota began to feel her cheeks flush. Maybe she was making a terrible mistake.

"That's fine. What day and time were you wanting to have your date arranged?" Elaine asked, unaffected by Dakota's shock.

"Wait!" Dakota erupted. "There's no um. . . you know . . . after the dinner . . ."

"You mean sex?" Elaine finished. "No ma'am. These arrangements are strictly platonic. Most women choose the date if they are attending an important event or party, and they don't want to go alone. You have to sign up for the Relationship or Marriage package if you want to have a physical relationship with your Real Man."

"Oh. . . That makes sense. Let me look at my calendar." Dakota fumbled with her laptop.

After Dakota scheduled her date, Elaine proceeded to ask her a series of questions regarding her dating history, lifestyle, and preferences for a partner.

"Do you get a lot of calls from women?" Dakota blurted in the middle of Elaine asking her a question.

"Of course! Over 90 percent of our customers end up purchasing the Relationship or Marriage package," Elaine said.

"Is this the future for women? Aren't there still good men out there?" If Dakota hadn't been inebriated at the moment, she wouldn't have asked this question. She wanted to laugh at herself and cry about the situation all at the same time.

Elaine's response shocked Dakota, "There will always be good people out there, but there aren't as many. Women are tired of waiting around or kissing all the bad frogs to find the prince."

"I see." Dakota sighed and closed her laptop. "But if a woman purchases the marriage package, she'll continue to age and look different but her partner will look the same. Am I right?"

"Our marriage package includes quarterly updates that will incrementally age your Real Man," Elaine explained.

"Wow. . ." Dakota finished off the rest of her wine. Her head was starting to throb, but she pushed through the rest of the questionnaire.

Now, a week after the phone call with Elaine, Dakota was sitting across the table from her Real Man. Their waitress had returned to their table with their dinners. After Dakota picked up a piece of sushi, she curiously watched Brad use the chop sticks and put a piece of sushi into his mouth. He chewed his food politely, unlike the other men Dakota had dated. It was a particular pet peeve of hers when people chewed their food with their mouths open. Table manners were particularly important to her. Dakota was starting to feel rather impressed by Real Man.

"I read on your profile that you play the viola in a symphony. That sounds very cool. Who is your favorite composer?" Brad asked.

"Oh gosh! It's impossible for me to pick a favorite. I love Beethoven, Ravel, Vaughan Williams . . ." Dakota was so excited to be asked a question about music. She could spend all day thinking and talking about the subject. "And I especially love Gustav Holst's *The Planets*. My orchestra is performing all seven movements in our holiday concert. Holst absolutely hated when orchestras didn't play his composition in its entirety."

Brad nodded thoughtfully. "*The Planets* catapulted Holst's career. It's kind of funny that he detested the fame that came as a result. Most people can only dream of reaching that kind of pinnacle in their professional career."

Dakota briefly lost herself in euphoria as she had never been able to talk about classical music with anyone. But then she realized that of course Brad would be well versed in the subject matter, since she had clearly specified in the phone interview that a moderate amount of interest in music was an absolute necessity.

They didn't just talk about classical music. Long after they finished their dinner and dessert, they continued to talk about movies and addicting television shows that felt like long-term relationships.

"When a TV series is over, it feels like a breakup. You spend so much time with those characters, they're like a part of your life," Brad said, and the two of them laughed.

"Do you think you feel love the same way as humans?" Dakota asked.

If Brad was offended by the question, he didn't show it. However, he took his time answering as though he were carefully thinking of the words he wanted to say.

"I don't think all humans love the same way, but I believe that love is the culmination of a journey you choose to take with someone. I think we naturally bond with certain people we meet along the way in life," Brad answered.

When they left the restaurant, Brad walked Dakota to her car. She felt an awkward moment when she didn't know whether she should shake his hand or give him a hug. He smiled, and suddenly all the thoughts in her mind were swept away.

She stuck out her hand, "It was really nice to meet you, Brad."

"I had a really good time. I hope you did too," he said.

Dakota nodded. "I have to admit, I didn't have expectations for tonight. In fact, I wasn't sure how this was going to turn out."

"Sometimes it's best not to have any expectations and just go with an open mind."

"You're probably right." Dakota smiled.

She got into her car and from her rearview mirror, she watched Brad cross the parking lot to his own car. When she looked back at her reflection, she almost didn't recognize her own smiling face. Her time with Brad was exhilarating and made her feel more alive than she had ever felt before.

Then she remembered he wasn't real. Her emotions split down two different paths. She had always imagined being in a relationship with another human, a real man, but now she started to wonder what was real anymore.

Dakota's fingers tapped the steering wheel. Nothing was

simple anymore, not even the definition of what was real. As she started the ignition, Dakota took one more look at Brad and then at her cell phone peeking out of her purse. Perhaps she should surrender to the evolution of humanity and embrace Real Man.

# A NOTE FROM THE AUTHOR

Thank you for reading my short story collection. As an author and photographer, I rely on word of mouth. If you enjoyed *The Stories of Our Lives*, please post a short review on Amazon and tell your friends.

If you're a fan of photography, check out my award-winning photography books, *Tattle Tales: Tattoo Stories and Portraits* and *Mannequins: Stories of the First Supermodel*.

Thanks so much!

## ABOUT THE AUTHOR

Brandy Isadora has always been an artist at heart. An award-winning author and photographer whose work has been exhibited internationally, Brandy believes that everyone has a story to tell. As a musician she travelled the world, and the people she met and the experiences she had inspired *The Stories of Our Lives*.

She is also the author of *Tattle Tales: Tattoo Stories and Portraits* and *Mannequins: Stories of the First Supermodel*.

 twitter.com/Brandy_Isadora
 instagram.com/Brandy_Isadora

www.ingramcontent.com/pod-product-compliance
Lightning Source LLC
Chambersburg PA
CBHW050302110726
47898CB00007B/2497